SECOND SEASON

MIA CLARK

Stepbrother With Benefits 9 is a work of fiction. Names, characters, places, and incidents either are the product of the author's imagination or are used fictitiously. Any resemblance to actual persons, living or dead, events, or locales is entirely coincidental.

ISBN: 1517256488
ISBN-13: 978-1517256487

Book design by Cerys du Lys
Cover design by Cerys du Lys
Cover Image © Depositphotos | avgustino

Cherrylily.com

DEDICATION

Thank you to Ethan and Cerys for helping me with this book and everything involved in the process. This is a dream come true and I wouldn't have been able to do it without them. Thank you, thank you!

CONTENTS

ACKNOWLEDGMENTS

Thank you for taking a chance on my book!

I know that the stepbrother theme can be a difficult one to deal with for a lot of people for a variety of reasons, and so I took that into consideration when I was writing this. While this is a story about forbidden love, it's also a story about two people becoming friends, too. Sometimes you need someone to push you in your life, even when you think everything is fine. Sometimes you need someone to be there, even when you don't know how to ask them to stay with you.

This is that kind of story. It is about two people becoming friends, and then becoming lovers. The forbidden aspects add tension, but it's more than that, too. Sometimes opposites attract in the best way possible. I hope you enjoy my books!

STEPBROTHER WITH BENEFITS

1 - Ashley

"ASHLEY, ARE YOU AWAKE?"

Nope! I'm kind of sleeping here? I guess I'm on the border between sleeping and waking up, but I just want to go back to sleep. I like cuddling in bed with Ethan. I like feeling his chest beneath my cheek and my arm draped over his body, and...

I can feel his slumbering erection with my knee, which is really exciting to me. I know that's kind of weird, but I like it. With my eyes closed still, I move my knee from the top of his thighs to a little higher, and nudge against his hard cock. He twitches as soon as I touch him, becoming even more aroused from the tiniest hint of stimulation.

Is he sleeping still, though? I wink open one eye to look and see, and he definitely looks like he's still asleep. His breathing is soft and his eyes are closed, but I suppose he could be faking it, too. It doesn't really matter, though, does it? I carefully sneak my hand down Ethan's chest, towards his stomach, a little lower. My fingers gently wrap around the shaft of his erection, and...

"Ashley?"

Oh my God. Oh no, no no. Um...

That's my mother. And she's upstairs. She's standing in the hallway, apparently. It sounds like maybe she's further down the hall near my room. I hear her knock on my bedroom door. I didn't leave it locked, because how would I get back in after? Ethan's door is locked, though. Which doesn't mean much, because if my mom opens my door she'll see I'm not there, and she'll know exactly where I am.

Just because... because, um... I can't think of a reason not to? I hold Ethan's cock a little harder, keeping a firm grip on him, and then I stroke him up and down. A little more. Faster and harder. He starts to wake up and his hips buck against my hand. He's so much more aroused in his sleep, and it's fascinating in a weird way. I did this before, um... *before* before. I got him to cum easily with just a few strokes when he was sleeping, and I didn't even know it was that easy, but apparently it is sometimes?

He's awake now, though. His eyes blink open, taking in his surroundings, and then he glances over at me. I smile at him, devilish yet sweet. Ethan grunts and settles back down onto his bed, then closes his eyes again. He puts his hands behind his head like he's relaxed, ready and waiting.

I feel him twitch a little more in my hands, and I think he's very close, which is exactly what I wanted.

"This is payback!" I tell him.

Which it is. For last night and his teasing. I'm allowed one tease, too, right? Rule number nineteen!

I let go of him fast right before he's about to cum and then I slip off the bed and run to his bedroom door. Before he realizes what's going on, I have the door open and I'm out in the hall.

Um... I don't know if I mentioned this, but I kind of forgot my clothes? I had them when I went into Ethan's room last night, but then I took them off. I still have my bra and panties on, which I guess is something, but it's really not a lot. It's especially not a lot when I almost crash into my mom in the hallway right outside Ethan's room. She stops and I stop and we stare at each other.

"Ashley!" my mom says, staring hard at me, her eyes narrowed.

"Um... hi, Mom," I say. "Good morning?"

"Don't you *good morning* me, young lady," she says. "Where are your clothes?"

Does she really have to ask that? Considering where I just came from, I think she has a pretty good idea.

"I was doing laundry?" I offer.

"I was willing to accept your relationship with Ethan," my mother says, huffy, hands on her hips. "Not if you're going to start lying to me, though."

I mumble and mutter something. My mom takes hold of my elbow and leads me down the hall to my bedroom, where she promptly opens the door and ushers us both in.

"Now, what were you saying before?" she asks, closing the door behind us.

"I left my clothes in Ethan's room," I mutter, quiet.

"That's all well and good," my mom says. "I understand that you and Ethan have... *interests* in each other that are easier to pursue without clothes on. I would recommend that next time you bring a pair of pajamas with you, though. What if it was your stepfather upstairs and you walked out like that? He's tolerant about a lot of things, but I don't think he'd appreciate that, especially since we haven't had that discussion together yet. He doesn't know about you and Ethan, and I would prefer he didn't find out by you gallivanting out of his son's room nearly naked."

Ugh. Yes... *ugh*! That would be weird. And gross. Kind of disturbing and awkward? I like

Ethan's dad, but that would be strange. He's seen me in a bathing suit before, which I guess is kind of the same idea, but I'm pretty sure he wouldn't appreciate it if I came out of Ethan's bedroom in the morning wearing a bathing suit, either, so...

"Sorry," I mumble. "I think we got a little carried away."

"Hey, what's with this *we* business?" Ethan asks, suddenly standing in my doorway. He opened the door and everything, just standing there, leaning against the wall, acting like he belongs there. "Little Miss Perfect over here is the one who came into my room last night and decided to start trouble."

"Oh, right, trouble. Is that what we're calling it now?" my mom asks. "You're not allowed in here right now, Ethan!" She gives him a half silly look, half glare, trying not to laugh at his nonchalant attitude. "My daughter doesn't have any clothes on, so get out."

"What? I've seen her without--"

But my mom's having none of it. She slaps at his shoulder and pushes him out the door. "I don't care, you! Go take a shower and pack up. We're going camping."

At least he was wearing clothes. I think that's good. Ethan thought this through better than I did, I guess. Did I really have to tease him like that? I could have slipped out of bed, put my clothes on, and then met my mother in the hall, but... *nooooo*.

I just had to try and be a bad girl, didn't I? I blame Ethan. This is all his fault.

"I don't care what he said," my mom says to me. "This is all his fault, dear. It's usually all the man's fault, too. That's why we're around to put some sense in them. Help them think rationally. I don't think I've ever had to have this conversation with you before, but most men are guided by... let's just say, impure thoughts?"

I stare at her blankly, blinking. "Mom, why are we talking about this?"

"It's all fun and games, Ashley!" my mom says. "It's all fun and games and sex and lust and everything, until my daughter comes barreling out of her boyfriend stepbrother's room half naked and--"

"Mom! Really?"

"Listen, dear," my mom says, quieter and calmer now. "I'm just saying that it's your responsibility to be the responsible one here. Ethan's the bad boy, and I think we both know you're a bit of... well, Ethan was probably right when he called you Little Miss Perfect. Are we on the same page here?"

"I really have no idea what you're saying," I tell her.

"I'm saying," my mom says, taking a deep breath, "behind closed doors, you and Ethan can be as naughty and crazy and wild as you want, within reason. I trust Ethan knows the limits there. He's probably been doing this long enough that--"

"Mom! Um... really?"

"I just meant that he has more experience than you, dear. That's all. There's nothing wrong with it, as long as he's serious and committed. I think it's fine, really, and--"

"Mom..."

"You're sounding a lot like my mother now, Ashley," my mom says, grumping at me. "I think I'm the mother in this relationship, don't you?"

"You're being weird, though," I tell her. And she is. *Ugh*. Weird.

"Here. Be quiet for a second. Go find some clothes to wear. Get some of the ones we picked yesterday," my mom says. I give her a funny look, but it's the first reasonable thing she's said so far, so I decide to go do it.

"I'm sure Ethan has a lot to teach you behind closed doors," my mom continues while I pick out clothes. "You can teach him a lot about being good out in the open, though. Like a gentleman, right? What I'm saying is if you're just skipping around in your underwear then who's going to teach Ethan to be a gentleman in public? Do you understand what I'm mean, honey?"

I grumble and mutter and I guess I don't want to admit it, but some of what she says makes sense.

"Alright, good," my mom says, even though I never actually agreed with her. "Now, how was it?"

"What?" I ask. "How was what?"

I didn't have a chance to hang up my clothes last night, and I didn't think I even needed to since

I was going to pack them this morning. I pick out a cute pink shirt and a pair of white shorts from the shopping bag I left on my bed, then hold them close to my chest, ready and waiting for her to leave so I can take a shower and pack.

"You know?" she says, giving me a knowing nod.

"Mom, I don't know what you're talking about," I say.

"The sex, dear? You had sex, didn't you? I just want to make sure you're having a nice time."

"Are you seriously asking me that?" I ask, blushing. Seriously, did she just ask me that?

"That's all I need to know," my mom says, smiling. "I'm glad you had fun. Now be prepared to be a lady today and to make sure Ethan's a gentleman, because we're all going to be camping and we'll have to figure out a way to tell your stepfather before you two are too..."

"You don't even know I had fun," I say. "Maybe we didn't have sex at all? Why are you looking at me like that?"

"Your cheeks give you away, dear," my mom says, smiling even more. "It's obvious, really."

"It is not!"

"Oh, yes, it is. Don't worry. Your secret is safe with--"

"Out!" I say, pushing her towards my door.

"Oh, shy now, are you? You go running out of Ethan's bedroom without any clothes on and you're perfectly fine, but when the conversation veers towards sex, you get embarrassed? It really doesn't make any sense to me."

"Mom..." I whine, pushing her towards the door some more. She opens it and grins at me, then lets herself out.

"Fine, fine," she says, waving her hand, dismissive.

"Oh, um... mom?"

The door is still open. She's just standing in the hall, grinning at me. When she sees the more serious look on my face, she settles into a regular smile, though.

"What's wrong?" she asks.

How does she know? I wish I knew. I don't know how to read people like that. I wish I did. My mom and Ethan and everyone else makes it seem so easy, but it's still hard for me to understand what other people are thinking.

She might know what's wrong, but she doesn't know exactly what it is. I tell her.

"Ethan's dad said some things to Ethan last night, I guess. It happened when they were shopping for tents and stuff. Um... they weren't talking about me and Ethan, but his dad said something about if he was my father, he wouldn't want someone like Ethan to date me, either. It's..."

What is it? I don't know what it is, and I'm not sure how to explain it, especially not to my mother.

She nods, knowing, and moves close to give me a hug.

"I understand," my mom says. "I don't think I agree with it, but I can understand why your step-father would say that. That's why this is important, alright? I know Ethan isn't a bad person, even if he's... well, we both know what he's like. You need to help him bring what's hidden inside him to the outside, so that everyone can see more of what he's like, though. I think his father knows, deep down, but he's worried, too, just like I worry about you, even though I know there's nothing to worry about."

"I know," I say, hugging my mom tight. "I don't want him to think like that about Ethan, though. He really is nice, and I know he's got a reputation for... for Ethan stuff. I don't think he's like that with me, though."

"Me either," my mom says, smiling and kissing me on the cheek. "You're smart, Ashley. If anyone can bring out the gentleman in Ethan, even if that gentleman is a little rough around the edges, it's you. Then when Ethan's father sees him with you, and sees it's because of you, he'll know. He'll accept it."

"Are you sure?" I ask.

"Positive," my mom says. "Let's not worry about that right now, though. You go shower and get ready, then pack. Lock your door, too! Don't let anyone in until you're ready to come out, under-stand?"

Her warning sounds dangerous. It really is, too. Do you know what would happen if I left my door unlocked while I took a shower, with Ethan Colton on the prowl after I teased him horribly this morning?

Um... I know exactly what would happen. It doesn't take a lot of imagination to figure it out. And, um... I kind of would not be opposed to it happening?

No! That's the bad girl talking, Ashley! Be the good girl you know you are, and um... bad girl things can come later.

My mom gives me one last hug before letting me go. Out of the corner of my eye, I see Ethan leaving his bedroom, hair wet, freshly showered, wearing shorts and a t-shirt. I hurry into my room and close my door, then lock it.

Don't even try it, Ethan! I know what you're capable of!

2 - Ethan

SERIOUSLY, HOW LONG DOES it take to pack for a camping trip? I don't think it should take that long. You know how long it took me to pack my stuff? About fifteen minutes. Maybe less. Yeah, I took a shower, too, and I brushed my teeth, got dressed, fixed myself up to look presentable. I'm not a slob or anything, I like to take care of appearances and look good.

I get that women want to look good, too, but this isn't about that. They're both showered, Ashley and her mom, and they're literally just packing now, nothing else, but they've been in the house for over an hour. What's up with that? Fuck if I know. It should be easy. Get clothes, put clothes in bag, get other necessities, put those in the bag, too, done. Pretty simple, right?

Nah, I guess not!

My dad and I are in the garage now, fixing everything up. There's the tents to deal with, fishing poles, some coolers of food that'll keep for awhile. We can get more when we're down there, but it's a good idea to pack a few bare essentials just in case. You never know, right? Don't want to go into situations like this blind and without a backup plan.

"Yeah, uh... Dad?" I say to him.

He looks over at me and grunts. "What's wrong?"

"Wouldn't it be easier if we took two cars? It's getting kind of cramped as it is, and who knows what Ashley and her mom have. I mean, fuck, they could both be bringing three or four bags. It's taking them long enough."

My dad gives me a straight look for a second, then he grins. "Would have been simpler with just us, huh?"

I grin back at him. "Yeah, I guess so. It's cool to bring them along, though. It'll be different, you know?"

"I remember the first time we went camping," he says. "That was horrible, but we made it work somehow. It ended up being a lot of fun. I don't know how. Honestly, after the first day I was considering packing everything up and driving back."

"Yeah..." I say, laughing. "It was kind of fucked up at first, but it was cool after."

"I'm sorry, Ethan. You know that, right? I know I've said it before, but it's the truth. I'm sorry about how I was back then. It just..." He trails off.

"Yeah," I say. "I know. Me too."

"Sometimes I think about it," he adds. "I don't know why. There was nothing I could have done about it. We tried. With your mother, I mean. We... we really did. I tried..."

"I know," I say. "I don't blame you or anything."

That was after my mother died. I was too young to realize exactly what was going on, I just knew that it was fucked up and it wasn't good. My dad tried to act like it didn't affect him, but how do you think that went? It's pretty hard. It was hard for me, and I didn't even know exactly what was going on. He was a grown man and had to deal with knowing the full details about everything.

That's not to say I agree with a lot of what he did. It wasn't even like he did anything obvious, he just... I don't know? Stopped caring? Not about me, just about life in general.

Yeah yeah, whatever. That's some depressing shit to deal with, and I don't want to do it right now. Thankfully I don't have to, because the women-folk just appeared.

"Hey!" my stepmom says. "What are you boys up to?"

"Just packing as much into the car as we can," my dad says. "I think it might be a good idea to follow Ethan's advice and take two cars, though. We'll have a lot more room that way."

"Alright," my stepmom says. "Whatever you two think is best. You're the camping experts here."

She smiles at my dad and he smiles back at her. They really do love each other, huh? It's nice. I'm glad. Good job, Dad.

Well, uh... then I do stuff. Yeah, let's go with that. I'm about to do some stuff. Say it, really, but whatever. Same thing.

"I can drive the second car," I say. "If that's cool with you."

"Sure, that works," my dad says.

Then, uh... "Ashley, you want to come with me?" I ask her.

She looks at me, confused at first, but then she smiles. Holy fuck, I love when she smiles at me. It's like Lady Luck herself, the sun, and every single star in the sky is shining down on me at the same time, beautiful as fuck.

"Sure," she says. "That sounds fun."

My dad gives me a weird look, as if I just told him I was going to renounce all mortal sins for eternity and become a chaste monk or something. My stepmom just smiles and nods at me, her little show of approval. Yeah, you know what? I'm a pretty fucking nice guy, don't you forget it.

"If you think you're up for the task, have at it, you two," my dad says.

"I think I can handle it," I say, giving him a nod.

"You want to use the old campground rules?" my dad asks me.

"Old rules, huh?" I say, grinning, mysterious. Ashley and her mom look at us like we're crazy, which I guess maybe we are. "I don't know. Do you think they can handle it?"

I give a quick jerk of my head towards the women, and my dad grins at them, conspiratorial.

"We can handle it!" my stepmom says. "Right, Ashley?"

"Um, I kind of want to know what we're handling first," she says, cautious.

Oh yeah, Princess? I've got something you can handle. Let's just go somewhere private first. I kind of want to say that, but my dad's right here, and uh... well, you know? Probably not a good idea.

It's my cock, though. That's what she can handle. My cock. I'm really good at this innuendo thing, right?

"Three out of four majority," my dad says. "Sorry, Ashley, it's old campground rules no matter what."

She mumbles to herself. It's kind of cute. I sort of want to go over and squeeze her tight and kiss her until she melts, but uh... yeah, my dad's still here. Can't do that, either.

"So what are old campground rules?" my stepmom asks.

"No technology allowed," my dad says. "Besides the cars, which we'll only use for the drive down there, as of right now there's a ban on anything electronic. This basically means--"

"Wait," my stepmom says. "I can't bring my phone?"

"Nope!" Ashley says, sticking her tongue out at her.

"This isn't good. What if I need it?"

"Mom, who do you even call? Me and Ethan's dad?"

"I might need to check the weather, though," she says. "How will I know if it's going to rain?"

"Look up? We'll be outdoors, Mom."

Ashley and her mom bicker back and forth. My dad and I just stand there, watching them, laughing. After awhile, we start to load some of the stuff we had into another car. It doesn't take too long.

"Alright, ladies. What do we have?" my dad asks them.

They each hold up a bag. One bag. Are you for real?

"Seriously?" I ask. "What took you so long to pack if you've only got one bag?"

"What are you talking about?" Ashley asks. "How many bags do you have?"

"Uh, one? It's just a camping trip, Princess. It's not like you need a lot. Some clothes, a bathing suit, a couple of towels."

"Wait, we need towels?" my stepmom asks.

"Mom," Ashley says. "You didn't tell me we needed towels."

"Are you two for real?" I say. "You took over an hour to pack and you didn't get towels?"

"Ethan, could you just go in and grab a couple of extra towels for them?" my dad asks me.

"Yeah, I guess. Give me your phones and stuff while I'm here. I'll toss them inside."

"What?" my stepmom asks. "I can't just keep it in the car when we're down there?"

"Too tempting," my dad explains. "It's easy to break the ban if you've got your phone right there. We always used to leave them here. There's phones at the campground, so it's not like we'll be completely without one in the event of an emergency. It'll be fine."

"But..."

"You're the one that agreed without even asking what the rule was," Ashley says, smirking. "Maybe next time you won't agree so easily?"

Yeah, you should always know what you're agreeing to, huh? Not sure it works like that all the time, though, Princess. Did you ever think we'd end up where we are when you first agreed to rule number one? I glance at her, just can't seem to stop looking at her, and she glances over at me, too. We look into each other's eyes and smile a little, but I don't think anyone but us realizes it.

Ashley reaches for her pocket, but then realizes her phone is in her packed bag. She opens the bag to get her phone, and I just stare at her. Fuck, those are some short, tight shorts, huh? I'm supposed to be taking this phone from her, but I can't stop staring at her legs. I kind of just want to lick them. Start at the toes and work my way up until I get to her sweet, creamy center... delicious as fuck, that's what that is.

Ashley's mom grumbles and hands me her phone, too. I guess I should stop staring at my stepsister's legs now? Yeah...

I take both their phones, and my dad's when he offers it to me, then I jog into the house to get some towels. I leave everyone's phone on the dining room table in the empty stone bowl in the middle where we keep fruit and stuff sometimes. I get some towels from the linen closet downstairs, then head back to the garage.

Everything's packed now. My dad and stepmom are getting into one car, and Ashley's standing by the other.

"You ready for the ride of your life, Princess?" I ask her.

"You think you're that good, do you?" she counters.

Thankfully my dad's in the car with the window up, so he can't hear any of this.

"Better," I tell her, smirking. "You don't even know what you're getting into here."

"I think I have a pretty good idea..." she says, grinning uncontrollably and winking at me.

My dad rolls down the window. "What's the hold up?" he asks.

"Nothing," I say. "Little Miss Perfect Princess over here was just whining about not having her phone."

"Stay strong, Ashley!" my stepmom says. "You can do it!"

Ashley rolls her eyes at her mom and laughs.

Yeah, well, that's it. Time for a road trip. We're going camping.

3 - *Ashley*

"ARE WE *THERE* YET?" I ask, tossing Ethan an antagonistic grin.

"Don't you even start with me, Princess," he says. He tries to sound angry, but he can't fool me.

I wait a few seconds before asking him again. "Ethan, are we there yet?"

"Oh, you want to play games?" he asks, laughing. "Don't make me pull this car over, baby girl."

"What would you do if you did?" I ask him. "Are you going to spank me? Huh?"

"What's with the spanking thing?" he asks. "You like that?"

I shrug. "I don't know? Kind of?"

"You either do or you don't," he says. "You can't be undecided about something like that. That's not how this works."

"I'm pretty sure I can be whatever I want about anything I want," I tell him, huffy. "I love pancakes, but I don't really like apple juice, even though I'll still drink it. That's the same, right?"

"So you're saying that you'd be into it if I spanked you, but you don't really care if I don't?" he asks.

"No," I say. "I'd probably really like it. It's just weird, don't you think? I mean, I don't want you to um... I don't know... I just like it when you grab me, and it just seems like the kind of thing you'd do after being grabby, right? Spanking, I mean."

"Yeah," he says. "I guess I get what you mean."

"Do you like it?" I ask him. "Doing it, I mean. Not um... not if I did it to you."

"Yeah, I don't think I'm really into the equal opportunity spanking, either," he says, smirking. "It was cool, though. I haven't really done that before like I did at the restaurant, but I liked it."

Oh, yes... the restaurant. I remember that *very* well...

We keep driving, lapsing into quiet conversation and mostly silence, just nice and relaxed. I stare out the window and watch the trees go by. We're on a country highway and the only car in sight is the one in front of us, the one our parents are in. Our parents can't see us or hear us, and it's just the two of us now. We can do and say anything we want. For now, at least. When we get to the campsite, I think that's all going to change.

"You've got your own tent," Ethan says. "Not sure if I told you that before, or if my dad did. I kind of almost told him that you and I could just share one, but he wasn't going for it."

"You *almost* told him?" I ask, raising one brow.

"Look, I did, I told him, but he said that wouldn't work. I didn't really try to fight with him about it, because for all he knows, it wouldn't work. From what I know, it'd work really well, though. Except tents are for sleeping, and if I'm in the same tent as you, I'm pretty sure I won't want to go to sleep, Princess. Maybe this is for the best."

"If you were in a tent with me, what would you want to do?" I ask him, coy.

He shakes his head, grinning, and sighs.

I sneak my hand closer to him, and rest it on his thigh. He glances down quick, looking at his leg and my hand, then he looks over at me, curious.

Acting innocent, I simply rub my hand back and forth, massaging his thigh. He shrugs and goes back to driving, paying attention to the road. I let him think that I'm not doing anything suspicious for a few seconds, and then I move into action.

My hand caresses up and down his thigh. Then in, towards his crotch, and, well... I squeeze a little. I can feel his cock twitch in response, tightening in his shorts. Ethan shifts in the seat, getting more comfortable.

"Hope you didn't forget rule number nineteen," he says, giving me a sidelong glance. "Don't start what you can't finish, Princess."

I grin at him. "You think I can't finish it?" I ask.

"Nah," he says. "You do whatever you want. Follow your heart's desires, remember?"

"You keep saying that, but you always say it when it's me trying to do something sexy to you," I say.

"It's pretty good advice," he counters. "Can't argue with the results, either. It seems to have worked out so far."

"For you," I tell him. "It seems to have worked out for you. First you get a blowjob, and now you're trying to convince me to give you a handjob while you're driving."

"I mean, why stop at a handjob?" he asks. "Go for gold, right? Go big or go home."

"Um..."

Was he saying what I thought he was? A blowjob... while he's driving? I don't even know how that works, except...

I take a quick glance at what I have to work with here. Ethan's seat is definitely far enough back that I *could* give him a blowjob, but he's driving, which I'm not sure is very safe. I guess giving him a handjob while he's driving isn't very safe, either, though. Doing any sex stuff while in a moving vehicle is probably not the safest thing to do, but I kind of want to do it. Do *something*. I'm not sure what yet.

I decide to do a little... just a little! Ethan is wearing shorts, so that makes this easier, too. I sneak my hand through the leg of his shorts and fidget my way up until I can feel his cock. Except he's wearing underwear. This isn't going to work. I tempt and tease him a little, still, caressing his ever-hardening cock with my fingers until I can see an obvious bulge in the front of his shorts.

I pull my hand back out, and Ethan grunts.

"So much for rule nineteen," he says. "Can't even follow your own--"

Before he finishes, I reach over and unbutton and unzip his shorts, then tug them a little down. Ethan lifts up his hips and helps me get them further. His foot gets heavier on the gas as he does, and the car engine roars a little louder.

"Ethan! Pay attention to the road!"

"I'm paying attention! What the fuck?"

"Well... be careful," I say. "If I'm going to do this, I don't want you to crash. We have to do this safe, alright?"

"I know how to drive," he says, glaring at me out of the corner of his eye.

"Oh yeah?" I say. "I know how to give a handjob, too. I've done it before."

"Who the fuck to?" he asks.

"You, duh."

"Yeah, I meant who else?" he asks.

"Um... no one else, really."

It's basically true, too. I can't say I didn't try, but it never really worked out. Now I'm kind of glad it didn't, either. It's weird, maybe, but Ethan is a lot more fun, if that makes sense. He's more interested in me and him and us together. I like exploring with him. I guess it's just me exploring, but I still like it because it's with him.

"Can I ask you something?" I ask him.

"Yeah, you literally just did," he says.

"Shut up," I say, slapping at his thigh. His partially freed cock twitches in anticipation. "I meant, um... is it always like this? Sex and relationships and stuff. Is it fun like this?"

"How am I supposed to know?" he asks. "You're the first girl I've actually dated, Princess."

"I know," I say. "That's not what I meant."

It's kind of weird to say, because in those regards I have more experience than Ethan? Except that's not really true, either. Yes, I've dated a couple of guys, but it wasn't very serious, and I want it to be serious with Ethan. He's never really dated, I guess, but he's... he's done things, which is kind of the same, but different.

"No, it's not always like this," he says. "Lots of guys are dicks, and they only think with their dicks. Don't get me wrong, I want to fuck you hard every chance I get, but I want you to have a good time, too."

"I'm not sure there's a lot of guys like that," I tell him, truthful. "I don't really know for sure, but it doesn't seem like it."

"It doesn't matter if there's a lot of guys like that," he says. "You're with me and I'm like that, so that's all that matters, right?"

I laugh because he makes it sound so simple. Is it, though? I guess it might be.

"I was just kidding before, by the way," he says. "Handjob in the car? Probably not a great idea."

I don't think I like that. I don't always like to admit it, but I'm kind of competitive, and I don't like being told I can't do something. It's not the same as Ethan, who just um... ignores all of that and does whatever he wants. It's more in an academic way, where if I know a class is difficult, I want to try harder to get a better grade. Or if someone says that freshmen in college almost never get special internships with the professors, I want to try harder to get one. I've always gotten good grades no matter what the class, and I even got a special internship for a few weeks my first year in college, so it makes sense that, um...

This is kind of the same, right? Except, no, not really. That's alright, though.

I reach over and pull at the waistband of Ethan's underwear with one hand, and reach past them with the other. I grab his partially erect cock, except it's more erect than I thought. It takes some work, but I manage to get it out and up and... well, it's very *up* right about now. Quite a lot of *up* is going on between his legs, actually.

I wrap my fingers around his shaft and stroke slowly up and down. He groans, his cock jerking and twitching in my hand, but he pays attention to the road and mostly seems to be driving safely.

"I'm not teasing you," I tell him. "I'm just going slow because I don't want you to crash or anything."

He smirks, but it's short lived. I stroke him a little quicker, and his smirk is replaced by an open-mouthed grunt of pleasure. It's really kind of sexy, actually. It's... I mean, I don't exactly listen to myself when I'm doing sexy things or having sex, but I know my moans are softer and um... more feminine, of course. Ethan's grunts are harder and kind of rough. I like the difference and the contrast there. It's like we're opposites, but we go together really well. Which... yes, we do. Very *very* well...

"It feels fucking amazing," he says. "For real, please don't stop."

"I won't, but be careful," I tell him. "I don't know how we'd explain this to my mom and your dad."

He grunts and nods. That's when I take deeper action and um... I don't even know what I'm doing. I'm just kind of making this all up as I go.

I shift in my seat and then lean over to the side, moving my head low. Ethan glances at me, confused for a second, except then I lick the head of his cock and he's not confused anymore. I take him quickly into my mouth, rolling my tongue around his cockhead while stroking him up and down. His hips move a little, almost bucking up, but he restrains himself.

I move back now, stroking my hand all the way up, then down to the base, bringing the recent wetness from my mouth and my tongue along with it. Up, then down... slow and steady. Ethan's cock grows even harder in my hand, the head a throbbing, angry purple color.

"Holy fuck..." he says.

"You like?" I ask.

"Damn fucking right I do," he says.

"Good," I say, continuing.

"Holy fucking... fuck! Are you for real? Seriously, what the fuck?"

This isn't anywhere near the same as before. If anything, it's the opposite. He sounds mad. I stop stroking him for a second and look where he's looking. It only takes a second to realize why he's mad. The forest cleared awhile back and we're driving through the outskirts of a small town, except our parents have decided to stop at a rest area. It's not much more than a gas station and a convenience store, but it means that we have to stop, too. Which means that I have to stop, which means...

It's pretty obvious what that means, and I'm kind of upset about it, too!

I stroke Ethan a little more until we slow down and pull over into the gas station, then I let him go. He shifts and pulls his underwear up, sort of covering his erection, but it's not exactly an easy thing to cover when it's like that.

He rolls down the window as he drives up to our parents. My mom rolls down her window, too, and Ethan's dad gets out of the stopped car.

"What's up, Dad?" Ethan asks. "Why are we stopping?"

"Need to fill up the gas," my stepfather says. "You two want anything while we're here?"

"I'll grab it," my mom says. "Unless either of you wants to come in with me? Do you need gas, too?"

I glance at the fuel gauge along with Ethan. "We're basically full," he says. "I filled it up the other day, and haven't really driven it since."

"My fault, then," Ethan's dad says. "I should have filled the tank right after we left. I didn't really think about it. You two go get a snack or something, though. It won't take long."

"Yeah, uh... about that..." Ethan says, glancing around. "Looks like there's a bathroom in the back. I'm going to go while we're here."

"Sure, sounds good."

Ethan rolls up the window and presses down on the gas again. He drives quickly towards the rear of the convenience store. There's certainly a bathroom back here--two, even--but he keeps driving past the doors and heads towards the rear of the back parking lot, mostly hidden from view of everything. We can see through the parking lot, and people can probably see where we're parked, too, but they can't see much unless they get close.

"Back seat," Ethan says. "Go. Now."

"Um, what?" I ask him.

"I'm combining rule number two and rule number nineteen," he says, like he's thought this through perfectly.

Which... I guess he has?

When I tell you to come here, you come here, and *we're only allowed to tease each other up to one intense moment of pleasure before the next time is the real deal.* Um...

He doesn't have to ask me, twice. I unbuckle my seatbelt and scramble through the middle divide between the front seats. There's not much in the backseat except my packed bag of clothes and his, but I toss them both onto the floor in the back and now we have all the room in the world. Ethan isn't far behind me, and then it doesn't take long for him to be in me, either. Honestly, I don't even know how that happened? One moment I have my shorts on, and the next moment they're pulled down to my ankles with my panties shoved aside, and there we go.

Ethan's very good at this bad boy thing, apparently. He knows what he's doing, and he does it very well.

He grabs my thighs and pulls me back, letting me slide along the smooth back seats. I'm laying sideways now, my head near one of the doors while my feet are by the other. I still have my shoes on and my shorts cling to my ankles, but it makes no difference to Ethan. He pulls down his underwear again, not even bothering to fully remove anything, and then he slips between my legs, and...

Mhm...

"Holy fuck, you feel amazing," he says after he thrusts inside of me. He holds himself there, filling me completely.

I gasp and wriggle against him. I... didn't expect this? I mean, I knew he was hard, and I wanted to give him a handjob in the car, but I didn't exactly expect there to be any reciprocation here. Not yet, at least. We weren't planning on stopping until we got to the campground, because it's only a few hours away. This is quite a welcome reprieve from the monotony of driving, though.

I wrap my legs around his waist and pull him even closer to me, deeper inside me. My arms cling to his back and I grab at his shirt. Ethan pushes down against me with his entire body and his lips latch onto mine, kissing me, frantic and obsessed. I kiss him back and grab at his upper body and pull him with my legs.

Yes, well... *yes*...

Ethan grabs me, too. He wraps his arms around me, holding me tight against him. Powerful, he pulls out of me, then plunges back in, out, then in... out, and in. It's harsh and fast, our bodies slapping together, the two of us slamming against the back seat of the car. He's not even trying to hide what we're doing and I know the car is rocking beneath the weight of our bodies and his thrusts. I slide my hips up to meet his constant, pounding cock, which only seems to intensify his sexual furor.

His lips are on my neck now, kissing and sucking. I tilt my chin back and the top of my head pushes against the back door of the car. Ethan reaches up and pulls my hair, pulls me closer to him. His other hand goes down and grips my hip, keeping me steady so he can better...

Fuck. That's what we're doing right now. Fucking, rutting, plain and simple, and oh my God it's the most amazing thing.

We've had sex in the car before. At the drive-in movie theatre, when I gave Ethan a handjob during the movie, we had sex then, too. That was careful and confined, though. I sat in his lap and we did it like that, trying not to alert anyone nearby as to what we were doing. We were supposed to be watching a movie, you know? Now, though, um...

This is not careful, nor considerate, nor confined. If anyone were to walk back behind the gas station convenience store for any reason, they'd see the car bouncing and they'd know exactly what was going on.

Our parents are here. My mom went into the store. Ethan's dad is pumping gas. Oh my God, this is either the best or the worst decision ever. I'm not sure which. I'm having a difficult time thinking right now.

I still have my panties on and every time Ethan thrusts inside of me, it makes the cloth ripple and shift against my skin, rubbing at my clit. It doesn't help that he knows what he's doing and his body presses and grinds against my core, too. I feel him throbbing inside of me, and then pressing against me, in, on, out, in...

"This is going to be quick," Ethan says, growling into my ear before nipping at my earlobe. "Sorry we can't take our time right now, Princess. I just needed to fuck you so bad. I want you to cum, though. Can you do that for me?"

I nod fast. "I... yes, I want to, Ethan. Please? Make me cum..."

Those are the magic words, apparently. His lips are on me again, kissing me. I kiss him back. I need to. I need this. I love the feeling of everything involving him. I love how he feels in me, how he feels on top of me, against me. I love how he makes me feel, like I'm sexy, but also sweet, how he's careful, but also rough. How he's...

He grunts and slams hard into me. I can feel him close, and I'm close, too. He's waiting, holding off, wanting me to cum so that he can. Oh... *oh yes...*

I squeeze hard against him, my pussy clenching against his cock, and he pulls out and thrusts into me again, as hard as he can. My body is caught between him and the seat, grinding against the two. He pulls out again, then slams into me one final time before giving in to his own orgasm.

It's all I need. It's enough. This isn't patient nor kind, but it's beautiful in its own way. My body gives in to Ethan's desires, and my own desires, too. Pleasure wells up inside of me until it's too much, and then my orgasm roars through me. I spasm beneath Ethan's muscular body and he throbs inside me, filling me with his cock and his cum.

We lay like that, clinging to each other, ecstasy overflowing inside us, shared between us.

I breathe heavily and let out a lusty gasp. "Oh my God, that was incredible," I say.

He laughs and kisses me fast, once, twice, three times, on my lips, my nose, and my lips again. "Fuck, you're beautiful," he says. "You know how amazing you look with my cock inside you?"

I laugh. "Really, Ethan? You're so strange."

"Nah," he says, smirking at me. "For real, you're beautiful all the time, but you're perfect like this. I wish I could look at you like this all the time."

"Oh, really, Mr. Bad Boy?" I ask him. "As far as I can remember, you're usually not paying much attention to how I look at all when we're having sex. What do you have to say to that?"

"Yeah yeah, so sometimes it's hard to see everything, but I can see what counts. I can see your face when you're about to cum, and your lips purse and your eyebrows scrunch up. Your nose wrinkles a little and you look so fucking intense and ready. That's all I need, Princess. I could watch you cum around my cock all fucking day."

"We, um... we don't have all day right now," I remind him.

"You're going to make me get up, huh?" he asks.

"I'm not going to make you do anything you don't want to do," I say, giggling. "Follow your heart's desire, right? It's just, um..."

Ethan tosses me one of his specialty bad boy grins, and moves off me a little to glance out the window. Then he freezes, mouth open, staring.

"Fuck," he says. "My dad's coming."

Oh no. Oh... oh no, oh my God. Ethan gets off of me and helps me up. I scramble away from him, trying to, um... my shorts. That's it. We need to get dressed. Fast!

"Dammit, Ethan!" I say to him, accidentally kicking his leg.

It's even more unfair because all he has to do is pull up his underwear and button and zip his shorts. I scramble to pull my own shorts up but there's not a lot of room back here. I shift and fidget and panic and hope that Ethan's dad doesn't see us, except I think he must see something because he's looking at the car weird. Thankfully we're in the back where the tinted windows are, and he can't see inside the car very well at this angle.

How long has he been there, though? He's walking towards us now, but if he's been there awhile he might have seen the car rocking up and down. It's also kind of probably rocking now, because honestly it's not exactly the easiest thing for two people to get dressed in the back of a car at the same time. Ethan's really not helping matters, either! I need more room.

I kick at him unintentionally again in my efforts to get my shorts back on. Alright, good, they're up, on, zipped, buttoned now.

We look like sex, don't we? It's that look that you have after just having sex, with messed up hair and glowing skin from the aftermath of exertion and orgasm. And, um... well, I guess it doesn't matter! There's not much we can do about it, now is there?

"I can't believe you did that," I say to him. "Seriously!"

"Did what?" he asks, grinning. "Give you an orgasm?"

"That's not even close to what I was talking about," I say, giving him a dirty look.

"Yeah, well, the orgasm was pretty great, huh?"

"Shut up. It doesn't matter how good it was because how do we explain this to your dad?"

"I wasn't planning on explaining your orgasms to my dad," he says.

"I hate you so much right now," I say, trying not to laugh.

"Love you, too, Princess," Ethan says, blowing me a kiss.

Then he opens the door and steps out of the car, just like that, doesn't even looks like he cares if we were caught. His dad is on his side, the driver's side, so they see each other immediately. Um...?

I get out of my side of the car and step out, too. Is this it, then? Is this when Ethan explains our relationship to his dad, because I'm pretty sure this is the worst time ever to do that. What's he even going to say? Yeah, hey, Dad, I'm dating Ashley and we just had a quickie in the back seat, no big deal, don't worry about it.

I wouldn't even be surprised if he said something like that, too. I kind of wish I would be, but I wouldn't.

Ugh.

4 - Ethan

YEAH, SO... MY DAD'S HERE. How's that for bad luck?

I guess I can't even blame it on bad luck, since I knew what I was doing. Just really hard to think when you've got an erection sometimes. It's just sort of like... hey, did you know you have an erection? This is your erection talking. Just had a public service announcement for you, buddy, and I could really go for thrusting into Ashley's perfect as fuck pussy right about now. Just in case you were interested, right? Because I know you are.

Yeah, me and my cock have conversations like that. They're pretty one-sided most of the time, because we basically agree on everything. Sex? Uh, yeah, sure, let's do it!

"What's going on?" my dad asks me as soon as I step out of the car.

"Something fell in the back seat," I tell him.

That's not a lie, right? Ashley kind of fell when she was scrambling to get back there, and I sort of fell on top of her. My cock fell into her pussy, too. More like I pushed it there, but when you push someone hard enough, they fall, right? That's basically what happened here. There was a lot of hard pushing going on, that's for sure.

Ashley gets out of the car, too, and stands there, quiet and wide-eyed. Fuck, this is bad. I get that she's nervous right now, but I kind of wonder what it'd be like to stare down at her when she's wide-eyed like that, sucking on my cock. I'll give you a surprise, Princess... just open your mouth for me, alright?

Stop it, cock! This isn't the time for that! Not that I even listen to myself, because I can feel a pretty fucking excited throbbing trapped in my shorts right now. Thank fuck I just came, or else I'm pretty sure I'd have a full on erection right about now. As it is, I've got that shit contained a little better.

My dad gives me a look. I'm pretty sure he doesn't believe me. To be fair, I don't think he believes me most of the time. Eventually he does, but he takes his time getting there. It's cool, I get it.

"Nothing broke, did it?" my dad asks.

Ashley shakes her head fast. "Nuh uh. Nope."

"Yeah, everything's fine," I say. "Kind of surprised considered all the flailing about Ashley was doing."

I toss her a grin and she stares at me, mortified.

"Uh...?" my dad asks.

"She was freaking out about her makeup or something. I was just trying to help her and she's over here screaming at me and grabbing my shirt."

Alright, so she wasn't exactly screaming at me. It was more of a moan, and only a few because we finished pretty fast. IF we took our time... yeah, I love making her scream. She did grab my shirt, though. That was pretty hot. Fuck, I've got to stop thinking about this, because I really can't get another erection right now. Calm down, bad boy.

My dad rolls his eyes at me. "Ethan, stop bothering her. Do we need to switch? Ashley, we have room in our car if you want to come with us."

"No, um... it's alright," Ashley says, trying to smile at him. "Ethan's just teasing me. I think I'm getting used to it. I'm pretty sure it's his way of showing affection or something."

My dad doesn't seem convinced. "Are you sure?"

She nods fast.

"Alright then, I guess." my dad says.

Just then, Ashley's mom walks around back, too. She heads towards my dad, then sees me and Ashley at the car, too.

"What's going on here?" Ashley's mom asks.

"Ethan was helping me since something fell in the back," Ashley says. "We were trying to, um..."

"Did you fall asleep in the car?" her mom asks her. "Your hair looks, um..."

It seems like no one can really say what's on their mind at the moment, and I'm sure not going to be the one to do it, so I'm out of here.

"Now that everything's all set, I've really got to use the bathroom quick," I say. "You all feel free to keep this conversation up, though. If you need me, you know where to find me."

"I've got to use the bathroom too," Ashley says. "Sorry for making everyone wait."

My dad gives me a funny look, and Ashley's mom gives me a funny look, then she gives Ashley one, too. I don't know what the looks are for. I go to the men's room and walk inside, just doing my thing. Ashley goes to the women's room, probably. Fuck if I know. She's not in here with me, at least.

I finish my business, go outside, start the car, and wait. Our parents are gone again. Ashley hurries to the car and gets back in the front passenger seat, then she glares at me and sticks out her tongue.

"What the fuck, what's that for?" I ask, making a face at her, too. You're not the only one who can make faces at people, Princess. For real.

"You almost got caught," she says. "I don’t even know how you'd explain that to your dad."

"Do I look like I give a fuck?" I ask her. "I just had sex over here. Real talk, Princess."

"I just had sex, too, Ethan!" she says, laughing and rolling her eyes at me.

"Yeah? How was it?" I ask.

"That's private information," she says. "I can't tell you."

"That's dumb."

"No, you are."

"What is this, kindergarten?"

"I didn't even know you in kindergarten."

"Wow..."

"Just drive!" she says.

I do. What else am I supposed to be doing? I pull out of the back and go to meet our parents in the front. They're ready to go, just waiting for us. I drive up behind them and follow them out when they pull back onto the stretch of country road that'll bring us back to the isolated highway.

"It was really good sex," Ashley says. "Is that what a quickie is? Is that what it's called?"

"Yeah," I say, looking over and smiling at her. "Usually I like to take my time, but sometimes you've just got to hurry the fuck up, you know?"

"I didn't know quick sex like that could be so fun, too," she says. "Um... can I tell you something?"

"You can tell me whatever you want," I say. "I'm here for you, Princess."

"I..." she hesitates, unsure. "I mean, I've had sex, um... I like sex with you the most, alright? But I've had sex and it was always fast before but it wasn't good like that."

"Obviously you like sex with me the most," I say. "Makes perfect sense. I'm a sex god."

"Shut up!" she says, glaring at me, trying not to smile.

"Nah, I get it," I tell her. "Listen, I'm being serious when I say I've never been with anyone like you before, and it's amazing. I'm sure you have opinions about my past and all, but I wouldn't lie to you about that. And, yeah, some guys are fucking dumb, and they don't care about anything but themselves, so there you go. That's what that's about. They just want theirs, and they use a girl's body to get it. It's stupid. I hate that shit. It should be about give and take, reciprocating, all of that. Everyone deserves as many orgasms as they want."

"Is that true, though?" she asks, giving me a weird look. I'm not really sure what this look is about, either.

"Yeah, some guys are like that. Probably most. Giving girls orgasms isn't always the easiest thing, but it makes you feel pretty fucking awesome, so I don't know why more guys don't work harder at it."

"No, um... not that..." she says, shy. "I meant the things you said about me? You've never been with someone like me? I... I still love you, though, Ethan. I'll still love you If I'm not the best or anything, because we have a lot of other good things, right? We still have fun. You still like being with me, um... you still like having sex with me, so that's all that matters, right?"

This really shouldn't piss me off, but it kind of does. We're driving, but I need to set the record straight with her. Kind of would prefer to sit her down and cuddle the fuck out of her while I do it, but that's not an option at the moment.

"Ashley, you're better than any girl I've ever been with. You're sexy as fuck, basically perfect in every way, you're smart, and I like that. You're cute and classy, but you've got a wild freak streak in you, too. It's not even just a small amount better, either. It's like, um... exponential or something. Exponential as fuck better by a lot."

"That doesn't even make sense," she says, grinning at me.

"Listen, it's like a hundred times better, alright? Is that good enough for you?"

"Just a hundred?" she asks.

"Fuck, a million," I counter.

"Just a million?"

"Greedy, much?"

"We should see if we can get the number higher, though," she says, nodding. "We'll have to practice."

"I will practice that with you," I tell her. "I'm pretty sure just by you saying we should practice, you're up to a billion times better now."

"You're cute sometimes when you say stuff like that," she says, smiling. Quick, she sneaks over and kisses my cheek while I'm driving. "You make it sound sweet, even though you're talking about having sex with me."

"Hey, it's not just the sex," I say. "What about cuddling? I've never even really cuddled with a girl before, but I fucking love cuddling with you. I'm romantic like that."

"Too bad we can't share the same tent, then," she says, pouting. "Just to cuddle, I mean."

"Yeah, of course, just to cuddle," I say, smirking.

"And having sex," she adds.

"Oh yeah?"

"And... talking?" she asks.

"I like sex and all, but if you ever want to cuddle and talk all night sometime, let me know. I'm down."

"Aw, really? That's sweet."

"Preferably naked cuddling," I add. Can't be too sweet here, you know? I need to keep up these bad boy appearances.

"I do like naked cuddling..." she says, grinning at me.

Aw yeah. I predict good things in my future. Hers, too. Ours, together. We've got to plan that shit together, you know? I'd like to have a future with her. Seems like it'd be the best.

5 - *Ashley*

WE'RE FINALLY HERE, and it's more amazing than I ever could have imagined. My mom and I aren't really the camping type. I think we both probably thought it would be fun, but when I was growing up, money was kind of tight, so we didn't go on a lot of trips. Camping isn't exactly expensive as long as you have all of the equipment for it, but getting the tents and everything was beyond us.

Not now, though. It's kind of strange to think about it like that, too. For Ethan and his dad, camping is probably one of the least expensive things they could ever do. It's a strange world to step into in a lot of ways, and yet I've stepped into it twice now, haven't I? First when my mom married Ethan's dad, which was sort of a shock that I'm still getting used to.

And now with Ethan. Is it going to be different because of that? Is dating him going to involve something else? Um... I don't think so. To be completely honest, Ethan doesn't exactly act like a spoiled rich kid billionaire playboy or anything, either. He just kind of does his own thing and lives his own life.

It's just weird to me, though. Camping is something relaxing and easy to Ethan and his dad, but to me and my mom the very idea of having enough money to go camping was an impossibility just a few years ago. Our vacations usually just consisted of spending the day at the beach.

It's beautiful here, though. I can see why Ethan and his dad like this place.

"What do you think?" Ethan asks me as we drive in.

"It's amazing," I say. "There's a lot of trees."

He laughs. "Yeah. Don't you worry, Princess. You'll have more than your fill of trees by the time we're done here."

"Can we go hiking?" I ask.

"You want to go hiking? You don't seem like the type."

I shrug. "I don't know? I've never been before."

"What? Are you being serious right now?"

"Um... yes?"

We stop at the main office, which is just a small building. The door is open and an older man and a boy probably about the same age as us come out to greet our parents. It's not much of a welcome, but they smile and they look nice enough. Ethan's dad talks to them first from inside his car, then gives them a piece of paper along with some money.

"Is it expensive to stay here?" I ask.

"Nah," Ethan says. "If you go camping with an RV, it costs a lot more, but with just tents and stuff it won't be too much. We're all on the same lot, so it's a pretty good deal with four of us, too."

"You and your dad used to just come here alone, right?"

"Yeah," Ethan says, kind of quiet.

Maybe he's thinking about something or remembering something? They've talked about camping before, but I don't really understand some of what they say when they mention it. It seems important somehow, but I don't know how.

Ethan's dad looks over his shoulder towards us and gives us a thumbs up from the car, then starts driving off again. We follow him. The road goes from regular to dirt and dust shortly after we leave the office. We drive through rows of trees, heading deeper and deeper into the forest. I can still see the main road from my side of the car if I look through the trees, but on Ethan's side it's all forest as far as the eye can see. We take a turn and go even further in. The road and civilization is behind us now. It seems so far away.

"I can see why you and your dad had those rules about leaving your phones behind," I say. "It feels like we shouldn't use them here, even if we had them."

Ethan grins. "Yeah. My dad kind of intentionally left out the fact that the signal's really bad here, too. Even if you had your phone, you probably couldn't use it for much. Could play games or something, I guess, but there's a ton of great stuff to do here, so I don't know why you'd want to."

"Oh?" I ask him, smiling, feigning innocence. "Are you sure there aren't any fun games you want to play with me?"

"You have no idea, Princess..." Ethan says, smirking.

It doesn't take us long to get to our campsite, even though it seems like it's forever away. It's far in the back, one of the last lots at the end of this dirt road, and with no one else nearby. In fact, it doesn't seem like there's a lot of people here at all. We passed a few, but nothing crazy.

Ethan seems to guess at what I'm thinking.

"It gets busier later in the season," he says. "The beginning of the summer is the time to come if you want to relax, though. We should have almost everything to ourselves. Just the way I like it."

"Why's that?" I ask.

"You," he says. "I've got plans, and every single one of them includes you and me, alone, nice and quiet. Not sure about relaxing, though. I'm going to make you real tired, Ashley. Hope you don't mind."

"Hmmm!" I say, grinning and thoughtful. Is he now?

We park our cars to the side of our lot. It's just a cleared out area for us to place our tents. I kind of like the fact that we can set it up however we like. It's sort of like building something. Not that we have a lot to build, but it reminds me of when I first moved in with Ethan and his dad, and how I got to plan out everything about my room. Um... now I just get to plan out exactly where my tent goes, but it's still kind of fun! It's different.

"Let's fight or something," Ethan says to me before we get out of the car. My mom and his dad are getting out and starting to pull their luggage from their car, too.

"What about?" I ask. "When are you going to tell your dad, by the way?"

Ethan shrugs. "I don't know. I want to try and look more responsible first."

"Um... so we're going to fight about something so that he doesn't catch on, but then you're going to try to look responsible so you can tell him we're dating?"

"Yeah?"

"What if we just don't fight, then? Won't that seem more responsible?"

"If we don't fight, that's going to seem suspicious," he says. "Yeah, I guess it might seem like it would be more responsible, too, but I doubt my dad sees it that way."

"I guess..." I don't know if I follow his bad boy logic in this, but it's his decision and if it makes him feel more comfortable, then I'm fine with that.

Also, I do kind of want to fight with him, because I have a good idea about how to do it. It's kind of a risk, and I don't think Ethan would like it if I told him beforehand, but that's exactly why I'm not going to tell him. He's the one that wanted to fight, right?

"Ew!" I say, loud enough so that my mom and stepdad can hear me. I get out of the car and glare at Ethan as he steps out, too. "That's gross, Ethan!"

He just gives me a weird look, like he's wondering what I'm even talking about. It's a good look, very convincing. Also, he really doesn't know, so that helps.

"Ethan? Really? What'd you do?" his dad asks.

My mom just looks at me, shaking her head. I'm pretty sure this isn't fooling her one bit, but I kind of like that, because I think she's going to really enjoy what I have planned.

I put my hands on my hips and harrumph. "He said that the lake was nice, and we should go swimming, except then he said I should wear my bikini, because it's, and I quote, 'sexy as fuck, Princess.'"

This is, um... I don't know? I'm trying to add motive! That's a thing, right? I think so, but I'm not really sure. Basically, er... I didn't really think this through too much, but I'm going to do it anyways. I have plans, alright? Just stay with me for a second.

I keep going. I can't stop now. "I mean, I guess it was a nice thing to say, but that's kind of weird, isn't it?"

Ethan shrugs, nonchalant. "Hey, if the bikini fits."

"I think the saying is if the shoe fits," I correct him.

"What the fuck do I care about shoes?" he asks. "Shoes aren't sexy as fuck. I've got priorities here, Princess."

His dad sighs. "Ethan, I know you like teasing Ashley, but--"

I interrupt him quick and turn to Ethan. "Do you think it's cute, though?" I ask him. "The bikini, I mean? I don't think I'm sexy. Um... Jake broke up with me, and... I'm not that kind of girl, Ethan."

I try to really play it up. This is like a good thing and a bad thing and I think this is going to work. It's a fight but then not a fight?

Ethan gives me a strange look as if he's trying to figure out what my game is in all of this.

"Cute can be sexy," he says. "Just a different kind of sexy. I didn't mean anything by it, Princess. It's not like I'm sitting here checking you out or staring at your ass all the time or anything."

Is that a lie? He stares at my ass? All the time? Um! How do I feel about this? I think I should be a little upset, but I kind of feel really happy about it if he does. Which he might not. He said he didn't, but the way he said it makes me feel like he does. I don't even know anymore.

"Is this what kids do these days?" my stepdad asks my mom. "Am I missing something here?"

"Oh, it's just some gentle teasing and rivalry," my mom says, waving her hand in the air, dismissive.

"Jake's a fucking idiot," Ethan says to me. This is real. Really real. "You're attractive, alright? Any guy would be super fucking lucky to be with you, and any guy who wasn't a huge asshole would treat you like a princess, so I don't know what's going on there, or what you two had together, but he's the one that's missing out. Understand? And, yeah, whatever, you do you, Ashley, be yourself, but if you want to wear that bikini of yours that I'm sure you brought, even though you're shy as fuck sometimes and don't want to wear it, uh... you find a guy at the lake and he's yours if you want him. Just make sure he's not a dick or I'll kick his ass."

Oh. Oh! I try not to smile too much, and I hold myself back from running over and jumping into his arms and kissing him over and over, but I really like that. I think maybe we're bad at fighting, though. Was this a good fight? Did Ethan's dad buy it?

I know it's kind of unorthodox, but I thought it might be good if we could fight, but then not fight, and also the motive, right? Ethan said I'm sexy as fuck, or I kind of lied and said he said that to start the fight, but, um... that doesn't matter! For all my stepdad knows, Ethan said it, and that's what counts, which means when Ethan tells him we're dating, it'll make sense. Sort of?

I don't know if this will work or not, but I love Ethan and he really is sweet sometimes, even though a lot of his sweetness seems to come with swear words and bad boy logic. I'm getting used to it, and actually I really like it.

"See?" my mom says to Ethan's dad. "I told you, didn't I? They'll be best friends by the end of the trip."

Ethan's dad seems skeptical still. "You might need to work on your approach, but it's great that you're looking out for Ashley," he says. "Just calm down with the four-letter vocabulary."

"Yeah yeah, got it, Dad," Ethan says.

6 - Ethan

I HAVE NO CLUE WHAT this girl is thinking, but I'm pretty sure she almost blew my cover. Seriously, who does that? I ask her to get in a fight with me to keep my dad from getting suspicious, and she tells him I'm talking about how sexy she is? What the fuck?

I guess it worked, though. Maybe. I still don't know what's going on there. I'm done with this. I've got work to do.

My dad and I pair off to set up the tent he'll be sharing with Ashley's mom, and Ashley and her mom are working on her tent. Theirs is a lot easier, but I think this is going to be awhile because they look like they have no idea what they're doing. My dad and I work pretty quickly, but this tent is sort of huge, so it's going to take some time. I'll help the ladies out after, though. Shouldn't be an issue.

"What do you think about Ashley?" my dad asks me.

I blink and look over at him. We're far enough away that Ashley and her mom can't hear us, but it's still a weird as fuck question to ask.

"It's been a few years since I married her mom and I was just wondering how you two are adjusting," he says.

"Is this about the sexy as fuck bikini thing?" I ask him.

"I don't know if that's a compliment nowadays or what, but I'm not sure it's appropriate for you to be telling your stepsister something like that," my dad says, grinning. "I admit it was kind of funny, though. I guess it's a nice thing to say."

I shrug. "Just trying to boost her confidence, you know?"

"Ah," my dad says, nodding. "I get it."

We keep working. This isn't complicated or anything, but there's a lot of technical work involved, holding shit up, putting everything into place. It's definitely a two man job.

"Are you two doing better, though?" my dad asks again. Apparently he can't keep this down.

"Dad, I don't know what you're asking, but I had a nice time hanging out with her while you guys were gone, so yeah, I guess we're adjusting or whatever you want to call it, and I guess we're doing better."

I'm not sure I want to say more. I feel like I'd incriminate myself. This is enough for now.

"What about that girl you're seeing?" my dad asks. "Ashley met her, right?"

Fuck. Uh... yeah... wow... how do I handle this one? Fuck if I know.

"We all hung out together a lot," I say. "You know, like swimming and all that. Watching movies. Pizza. Whatever the fuck."

"I don't think doing 'whatever the fuck' is an actual activity, Ethan," my dad says.

"Sorry. It's a bad habit."

"It's fine. I'm used to it. Let's just try to calm it down in front of the girls, alright?"

Yeah... I'm anything but calm around Ashley, though. You think I say "fuck" a lot, Dad? Pretty sure if I had the opportunity, I'd be doing it with Ashley a whole lot more than saying it. But what do I know? Going to have to calm that down, too. I doubt that's kosher what with uh... yeah, these tents are only going to be twenty feet apart, if that.

Can you keep quiet at night, Princess? If I sneak into your tent, you promise not to moan too loud? Because, you know what? I don't think you can keep that promise, and I'm going to do everything within my power to make sure you don't, so...

My dad gets a hammer to pound one of the corner stakes for the tent into the ground while I hold up this side and have impure as fuck thoughts about my stepsister. Also, I look over at her, too, because I kind of want to check out her ass. Sexy as fuck, that's what that is.

I can't see it, though. I can see her just fine, but not her ass. Her and her mom are talking quietly about something or other, I don't even know. The tent isn't going up very well, but I have a sneaking suspicion they aren't even trying anymore. Yeah, yeah, don't worry, we'll come save you two damsels in tent distress. I'll rescue you, Princess. Just call me Ethan, the tent-slayer. I get that this makes no sense, but whatever. I'm busy holding this tent, and I'll help them out after.

Except Ashley's got other plans. I knew she was smart, but I didn't realize the full extent of it, I guess. I sort of just figured she used her powers of intelligence for the greater good, you know?

Nah. This girl is devious as fuck...

She notices me watching and winks at me, then holds a finger up to her lips, telling me to keep quiet. You got it, Princess. No words from me. She sneaks over to the firepit we set up before, where my dad left his spare hunting knife. He was just using it to scrape shavings from a piece of wood so he could light a fire easier later.

Ashley doesn't care about the fire, or proper knife usage. She slinks back to the tent, all while me and her mom watch her, and then she pokes through it. Yeah, uh, what the fuck? Slices right through the tent, then tosses the knife back towards the firepit, and pulls the tent apart. The sound of it ripping practically roars through our campsite, catching my dad's attention. He's done pounding that stake in and he jumps up and looks at me.

"What was that? Did the tent rip?" he asks.

I shrug. "Nah, not over here."

"Oh no!" Ashley says, super exaggerated.

She stares at the tent, and her mom does the same thing. They both look crazy to me. These crazy women are just stabbing and ripping tents. Seriously, who does that?

"It ripped..." Ashley's mom says, sounding devastated. She is totally not even devastated. They planned this. These people are insane.

"What?" my dad says, buying into it. I don't want to say he's gullible, but, uh... if the bikini fits? Yeah, I think shoes are a better choice here. Ashley was right.

He rushes over to inspect the tent they were working on, and sure enough it's ripped. I could have told him as much, because I saw it happen, but whatever. I go over, too, just because I feel like I should. Someone's got to bring back the sanity, right? Never thought I'd see the day when it was me doing it, though.

"We've only got two tents now," Ashley says, sort of frown-pouting. I don't know what you call that, but it's cute as fuck.

"This is bad," her mom says. "What do we do?"

You don't stab and rip your tent! Duh!

"It's too far of a drive to get a new one here," my dad says. "I guess we're going to have to share. How about this? Ashley, you and your mom can take the tent that we were going to use, and Ethan and I can share his tent."

"Oh! Oh, no no no," Ashley says, shaking her head fast. "I wouldn't want to do that."

"What do you want to do, honey?" her mom asks her.

I mean this in the nicest of ways. I'm not saying this out loud. I'm not calling Ashley and her mom a bitch, so please don't take this the wrong way, but...

Yeah, for real, these crazy bitches planned this out. They planned all of it out. Complete fucking insanity, that's what this is.

It's working, though. Holy fuck. They're too smart.

"What we should do is you two still share a tent like you planned," Ashley says, nodding to my dad and her mom. "Then Ethan and I can share his tent?"

"Do you think that's a good idea?" my dad asks, brow furrowed.

"It's a pretty big tent," Ashley says.

"They are a good size, hun," her mom says to my dad. "I'm sure there's more than enough room."

Well, fuck, why don't I just join in on this?

"Yeah, I picked them out because we'd have some room to stretch," I add. "Mine's the same size as Ashley's, and both were bigger than the tent we used to share way back when, Dad. It's not like I wanted to share a tent with her, but I guess it can't be helped."

It could have been helped. It completely absolutely definitely, no fucking doubt in my mind could have been helped. It could have been helped if they just didn't plan on ripping the tent.

Yeah, whatever. Who am I to complain? I just got easy access night visits with my secret girlfriend over here. Aw yeah!

Good job, Ashley. I knew I was dating you for a reason. You're pretty fucking smart.

She winks at me and I smirk at her while my dad inspects the rip in the tent. My stepmom smiles and holds a finger to her lips; this is our secret, I guess. Don't tell anyone. Secret secrets.

My dad looks up and sighs. "As long as it's not a problem with you two. If it's too much and you want some space, we can switch, though. Ethan said you two have been hanging out while we were gone, though, so maybe this'll be fine, too."

"Did you know he made her soup last week?" my stepmom asks. "Ashley wasn't feeling well the day before she went to visit her friend, and Ethan made her soup and they watched a few shows on Netflix. Isn't that sweet?"

"Yeah?" my dad asks me, one brow raised.

I shrug. "I felt bad," I say. "I was kind of sick the week before coming home for the summer so I figure she must have caught it from me. I thought I should make it up to her."

"It was very nice of you, Ethan," Ashley says, prim and proper.

This girl was not prim and proper last night when she was using a sex toy on herself while sitting on my cock, that's for sure. Now she's just

Little Miss Perfect Angel, though, huh? She's pretty good at this, I'll give her that.

"I guess it's decided, then," my dad says, clapping me on the back. "If you change your minds later, just let me know. If Ethan snores too much, you can switch, too."

"Ethan doesn't snore," Ashley says, confused.

Holy fuck. Seriously? Really really? I take it all back. I thought she was smart, and then she goes and says something like that. Yeah, explain to my dad how you know I don't snore, Princess? Go right ahead and tell him we've slept in the same bed for over a week now, so you know exactly what I do and don't do at night? Why don't you just go ahead and tell him about my morning erections while you're at it, too? Good idea, right?

My dad's oblivious, though. "I was just joking," he says, laughing. "Hopefully you two will be fine! It's just sleeping, right? The rest of the time we'll be out and about and enjoying nature."

Yeah... about that *just sleeping thing,* uh... I do not think so.

7 - *Ashley*

MY PLAN WORKED! Twice in a row! I'm very good at *bad* plans, I guess. Bad girl plans, I mean. Naughty ones, like how to share the same tent with my sexy boyfriend without his dad realizing my ulterior motives.

And I did it without even giving myself away or looking suspicious! My mom helped. It was kind of partly her idea, too. We shared the plan.

The tents are set up now and everything's good to go. It's getting kind of dark, though. We got here later in the day, and we probably still have a few more hours until it's completely night out, but it's definitely evening now. My stomach grumbles, and everyone looks over at me.

"Hungry?" my stepdad asks.

"A little," I say. *A lot!*

"We can get some more food tomorrow, but how about hot dogs for tonight? They aren't fancy, but they're easy and they should get the job done."

"I like hot dogs," I say, smiling.

I know they aren't exactly good for me, but I used to have them sometimes when my mom worked late before she married Ethan's dad. Hot dogs and french fries while I watched TV after finishing my homework.

"I'll go find some sticks we can skewer them on," Ethan says. "You ever roasted your own hot dog over a fire?" he asks me.

"Um... no?"

"It's fun," he says. "The real camping experience. Everyone should give it a try at least once."

I smile at him and he smiles back at me. I know we aren't doing anything extreme or intense or extra exciting, but I like this still. The experience is fun, and it's so different from anything I've ever done before. Almost everything with Ethan is so different from anything I've ever done before.

While Ethan scavenges for sticks we can use to skewer the hot dogs, the older man from the office comes hiking up the road towards us. The younger boy about my age is walking alongside him. The older one waves as he approaches. The one my age keeps his hands in his pockets, but he smiles and nods at me.

"Hey, John," Ethan's dad says.

The older man nods. "Howdy, folks. Just checking to make sure everything's going alright. I didn't get a chance to meet you all earlier, so I wanted to stop by."

Ethan's dad smiles. "Sure. You met me and my wife earlier, but that's my son, Ethan, and my daughter, Ashley."

That's how he usually introduces us, saying I'm his daughter. It's a simpler introduction. This isn't exactly strange or anything. It just, um... it feels kind of strange now, because of what Ethan and I are doing. I know my stepdad doesn't know, but it makes me a little uncomfortable still. I fidget and shift side to side, nervous.

John waves to us all. "Great to meet everyone. This is my son, Caleb. I'm always up at the office if you need me. Caleb does work around the campground sometimes, but he's not an official worker here. You might see him hiking or swimming, too. If you need anything, you can let him know, though. We're always happy to help."

"Yeah, definitely," Caleb says, looking right at me. When our eyes meet, he glances away, sort of shy, but determined.

It's cute in, um... it's cute, but I'm with Ethan. He seems nice, though. I glance away and look towards Ethan, who is giving me a strange look.

"I don't want to take up too much of your time, but there have been some reports of howling in the woods the past week or so. It's just rumors so far and we haven't seen wolves around these parts in forever, plus nothing's confirmed, but it's always better safe than sorry," John says. "I assure you there's nothing to worry about, and the forest ranger keeps a close eye on all the campgrounds in this area. Just make sure you clean up everything and dispose of your trash as soon as possible."

"I do trash runs every day," Caleb adds. "There's barrels up at the office. As long as you bag your trash up, I don't mind taking care of it if you see me passing by. I'm usually around here a lot."

Everyone nods, but I keep nodding even more. Caleb doesn't seem like he's talking to anyone but me. I blush and look away, and he does, too. Um... is he flirting with me? It's not like how Ethan flirts with me, so I'm not really sure. I don't know if I've been flirted with before, to be honest.

Ethan's dad grins when he sees us like that. Like what, though? I have no idea. I'm kind of confused here.

"Ethan and I have a good amount of camping experience," my stepdad says. "We'll make sure to keep everything cleaned up, hang the trash up at night if we have to, or just bring it to the office. You don't have to worry about anything. Ashley's new to camping, though. She just broke up with her boyfriend, so we thought it'd be nice to come here and relax, just get away from it all and have a nice time."

Caleb's ears perk up, and he looks at me again. Um... I don't think... why did Ethan's dad say that...?

"You should come back during the day if you want," my stepdad says to Caleb. "I'm sure Ethan and Ashley wouldn't mind some company their own age to hang out with, right?"

"Sure?" I say. I don't know if that's a yes or a no.

Ethan glares. At something or someone or everything and everyone. He grumbles, but I'm not sure what he's saying.

"You *were* talking about the two of you going swimming before, weren't you?" Ethan's dad asks him.

Oh... oh my God. What's going on? He did say that. Ethan also said my bikini was sexy as fuck--sort of, actually I said that he said that, but that doesn't really matter--and that any guy would be lucky to be with me, and if I found a guy at the lake, he'd be mine if I wanted him, which...

I'm pretty sure Ethan was talking about himself. And that's who I was thinking of when he said that. Obviously his dad didn't know that, though. His dad definitely didn't know that, and now he's trying to tell Caleb to go to the lake with me, for...

Oh my God, he's trying to set me up with the campground owner's son. I don't know why this is so surprising to me, but it is. I'm just... I'm not good at these things. Flirting things? I don't want to be good at them, I don't think. I do, but with Ethan. Except Ethan's dad doesn't know that. We haven't told him yet. What am I supposed to say?

Nothing, I guess.

I mumble and murmur to myself and blush and fidget and Ethan glares and seethes, but

Ethan's dad is oblivious. My mom is trying to deflect, I think. I'm not actually sure what she's doing. John and Caleb are leaving, though.

Good. I think. Is that good? I don't know what's going on or what I'm supposed to do anymore.

"See you later, Ashley," Caleb says, waving to me before him and his dad leave. "Was nice meeting you."

I nod and try to smile and wave a little, but I think maybe I look like a blushing, nervous idiot.

"I don't want to hang out with that kid," Ethan says to his dad as soon as John and Caleb are out of sight. "I thought we came camping to have some family time or something?"

Ethan's dad shrugs. "You don't have to hang out with him, Ethan. It looked like he'd rather hang out with Ashley alone, anyway."

I don't know what's happening, or what's about to happen, but Ethan looks pissed. His face is kind of red, and he has all of the sticks for our hot dog skewers in his hand, but the way his fingers are clenched and turning white, I think he's about to snap them in half whether he wants to or not.

My mom goes over to him and whispers something into his ear to calm him down, then she gives him a hug. Ethan loosens up a little, but doesn't hug her back. He gives her the skewer sticks, then stomps over to the woods to cool off, I guess.

"I don't get it," my stepdad says.

I do. I want to go after Ethan, but I'm not sure how or what I should say. I can't really do much with his dad here. I wish we could tell him, but I'm not sure we can right now. I don't know what to do.

The decision is made for me.

"Ashley, do you mind heading up to the office and filling this water jug for us?" my stepdad asks me. "I saw a pipe and faucet next to the building. It's just sticking up out of the ground, for public use. I was going to ask Ethan, but I guess he wants some alone time. Sorry about that."

"Oh, no, I don't mind," I say. "I can do it."

8 - *Ashley*

THE WALK TO THE MAIN OFFICE is really nice. I take the scenic route part way, just following the road we drove on to get to our campsite instead of skipping through the woods. There's not a lot of people here right now, and it's mostly empty except for us. I wonder if that's partly because of the wolf, or if it's just because of the season. I know Ethan said more people go camping in the middle of the summer instead of right at the beginning, but maybe this is just a quieter place in general, too. It did take awhile to drive here, but it seems nice and well worth it.

I skip through some of the campsites instead of following the winding road all the way back to the front. The road's nice, but I kind of want to hurry and get back. Maybe I can talk to Ethan privately, or maybe we can go for a walk? Maybe not, since it looks like we'll be having dinner soon, and it is getting kind of late today. The sky is darker, though not completely dark yet. I breathe in deep and take in the fresh, forest air. It tastes different than I'm used to. I don't think I've ever actually spent time in the woods before this. We have some parks back home, and also at school, but nothing like this wide expanse of trees and forest.

It's exhilarating and interesting in an entirely new way. I'm not really sure how I fit in here, but I like it. I'm not exactly the outdoors type of girl, if you know what I mean? Some girls are really sporty and seem like they'd fit in a place like this more. I try to stay active and I do exercise a little, but if I got lost in the woods, um... I'd be lost. I feel kind of lost already.

I reach the office after a decent trek, maybe ten minutes or so, and it doesn't take me long to find the water faucet. It's just like Ethan's dad said, just a pipe coming from the ground next to the building. The lights are on in the office, so John and Caleb must be there, but the faucet's in the back so I don't see them.

This jug is kind of huge, though. I knew that when I took it, but I didn't think about filling it or taking it back with me. It's one of those big gallon ones with a twist off top and a spigot at the bottom. I take off the top and put it under the faucet, then turn the water on and wait for it to fill up.

"Hey," someone says right next to me.

I jump. "Ohmygod!"

I almost slap the person, but he steps back quick and catches my hand in his. He laughs at me, and I just keep staring, surprised.

"Caleb, you scared me," I say, smiling now. It's kind of funny. That really shouldn't have scared me, but I wasn't expecting it.

"Sorry," he says.

We're still holding hands. Sort of. He caught mine and I didn't pull it back, and now our hands are dropped in front of us, kind of a cross between holding hands and shaking them.

I've never really held hands with anyone before. I tried to hold hands with Jake back before I found out what a jerk he was, but he always pushed me away. He said he didn't like public displays of affection. I'd love to hold hands with Ethan, but we have a similar issue going on. A lot of people back home know that we're stepbrother and stepsister, so it seems kind of weird to hold hands out in the open. I'm not sure if people would judge us now.

This isn't really the same thing, but now I'm holding hands with Caleb, and...

I just kind of imagine it's Ethan for a second. Not really, because Ethan and Caleb don't even look the same. Caleb is cute in his own way, though. Not um... I'm not checking him out, alright? I'm just saying that I bet he has a girlfriend or something, because someone that looks like him probably does. Granted, someone who looks like

Ethan could probably have a girlfriend, but he didn't until me, so what do I know?

What if Caleb is like Ethan? A bad boy player, who has quick flings with girls and then ignores them? Or what if he's the good parts of Ethan: sweet and considerate, a little careful and a little rough?

Why am I even thinking about this?

We've been holding hands for awhile now. Awkward or what? I try to extract myself from this weird situation, but it's not exactly working. I think Caleb has realized it, too, because he makes some lame attempt at shaking my hand to shake the awkwardness off as an introduction or something. I don't know.

I smile at him, sort of forced, then check the jug. It's only halfway full. Ugh.

"I didn't think I'd see you again this soon," Caleb says.

"Yeah, I'm just getting water," I say.

"That's a big jug," he says. "Do you need help bringing it back?"

"I should be fine," I say.

I actually could probably use help, but I don't think that's a good idea. What would Ethan think if I came back with a guest? No... not a good idea at all.

We're silent for awhile, neither of us talking. I stare at the water, willing it with my mind to fill up faster. I'm the smart good girl and all, but apparently my psychic abilities haven't manifested yet.

They make it seem so easy in the movies, don't they?

"So, you broke up with your boyfriend?" Caleb asks.

"He broke up with me," I say, correcting him. "Right before I came back home for the summer. He's kind of a jerk, to be honest. I just didn't realize it at first. It's not a big deal."

Why am I rambling like this? Why am I telling this strange boy my entire life's story? I have no idea!

Then I say something stupider while trying to stop saying stupid things. "Do you have a girl-friend?"

Yeah, um... I'm smart with grades, stupid with people. Who asks something like that? Someone who is interested in whether the cute boy who is showing interest in her is actually interested and available, that's who. Which isn't me. I'm not interested, and I'm not available, either.

I'm not exactly uninterested, though. I don't want to be mean about it, you know? I just don't want him thinking I'm trying to put the moves on him or anything. Honestly, I have no idea how to put the moves on anyone. Is that something girls can do? I don't even know.

"No," Caleb says. "Haven't found the right girl yet, I guess."

That's an answer. It's definitely an answer. Alright, then. Good. Um...

Why do I feel so awkward? I still don't know if he's flirting with me. This isn't at all how Ethan flirts with me. Is that what it's called, though? I thought I knew what flirting was, but honestly I have no idea. Am I flirting back? I don't mean to be if I am. Maybe I should just tell him that? Just so you know, Caleb, I'm not flirting with you...

"How long are you going to be here?" Caleb asks.

"Um... just a week or two, I think?" I say. "I'm not sure yet. We're kind of playing it by ear, I guess."

"Cool, cool," Caleb says. Silence again, for a little while. "Hey, we should hang out sometime or something."

He's moving closer now. He's leaning towards me. Why is he looking at me like that? Is he going to kiss me? What do I do? I mean, I know what I do, sort of. I don't let him kiss me, that's what! I think?

I don't know how any of this works. I feel safer and better with Ethan. We have rules, and an understanding, and it's not like we *need* the rules, but I like having them. I know where I stand with Ethan, if that makes any sense? I know what we are, and even though I don't always know what he's thinking, I just...

I don't even know Caleb! He can't kiss me! That's just weird. I'm sure he's a good kisser and all, but... wait, Ashley, why are you thinking about what kind of kisser he is? That's not even important. It's...

"What the fuck are you doing?"

Oh, shit, that's Ethan.

Ethan comes up and pulls Caleb away. Who, apparently, was not trying to kiss me. The water jug was about to overflow and he was leaning forward and reaching out to turn it off. I don't even know how I misconstrued that as kissing, except apparently Ethan thought so, too, or thought *something,* at least.

Ethan jerks Caleb away from me and the water. I reach down to turn off the faucet myself, and then grab the top and twist it back on. Everything is all set. We can go now. We can leave.

Maybe.

"What's your problem, man?" Caleb says to Ethan.

"Me? What the fuck are you getting so close to Ashley for?" Ethan asks.

"We were just talking. I was helping with the water."

"Look, dude," Ethan says, "She's not stupid. She knows how to turn the water off. This girl has always had perfect fucking grades, so don't treat her like an idiot."

"What are you talking about? I wasn't. Like I said, I was just trying to help."

"Ethan," I say. "It's fine. Really. Caleb was just being nice."

It looks like they're going to fight. I'm pretty sure Ethan would win, but I don't want to see the outcome of a fight, regardless. I don't know what would happen, either. Would we get kicked out of the campground for fighting with the owner's son?

Worse yet, would Ethan's dad make Ethan leave without us, since he was the one starting trouble? I don't want to be here if I'm not with Ethan. I'm sure camping is fun and all, but it just wouldn't be the same.

Ethan and Caleb have a stare down. I'm not sure who's winning. Boys and their stare downs kind of confuse me. Ethan grunts and looks away first, then grabs the water jug, hefting it up in both his hands, holding it close to his chest. Caleb softens as soon as Ethan looks away, relieved.

"Let's go," Ethan says to me. "I don't know what my dad was thinking sending you here to do this. He should have just asked me to do it. This shit's heavy."

"I can carry it," I say. "You didn't have to come and help me."

He looks at me, and it's the same expression as before, nothing different, but there's something in his eyes that seems hurt? I don't really know. I didn't mean to hurt him.

"Look, I didn't mean to start any trouble before," Caleb says. "I get that she's your sister and some guy just broke up with her, so you have a right to be protective. I was just trying to help, that's all."

"It was nice of you, Caleb," I say, hoping to defuse this situation before it gets bad again. "Thank you."

Ethan grunts, but doesn't say anything. He starts walking back to our campsite.

Without me. He doesn't even say anything to me, doesn't even wait for me, he just walks away. What the heck?

"See you later, Ashley," Caleb says, smiling. "I'm sure I'll see you around."

"Bye, Caleb," I say, waving to him before hurrying after Ethan.

We walk side by side quietly for awhile. I'm not sure if I should say anything, but, no, I'm going to say something! He can't just do those things, and act that way, and be a huge jerk for no reason, you know?

"What's your issue?" I ask him, rather forward.

"*My* issue?" Ethan asks, indignant.

"Yes, yours."

"Listen, Princess," he says. "It's him. That Caleb dude whatever. I don't like the way he's looking at you. He's obviously got a crush, and then my dad saying all that shit before. It just pisses me off, alright? Are you happy now?"

"I'm not happy, Ethan," I say. "It's not like I wanted your dad to say that. I'm not trying to flirt with Caleb, either. You don't have to--"

Worry about anything. That's what I was going to say, but Ethan stops and stares at me.

"Hold up, was that guy flirting with you?" he asks.

"No!" I say. "I mean, I don't think so? I'm not sure."

"What the fuck, how do you not know if someone is flirting with you?" he asks.

"I'm not as experienced a flirter as you!" I counter.

We're yelling now. It's not the loudest argument ever, but it's pretty loud. I think it seems louder because it's just us in the middle of the camp woods. Thankfully no one else is around us. I hope no one hears us.

"Do you *want* him to flirt with you?" Ethan asks. "Is that what this is about?"

"Is that what what's about? You aren't making any sense. Also, every girl likes compliments, so if that's what he was doing and if that's what you consider flirting, then, yes, I like that."

"Holy fuck," Ethan says, shaking his head. "I compliment you, you know? I flirt with you. If that's not enough for you, I don't know what the fuck to say."

"I didn't say that! This isn't a competition, Ethan. I don't even think he was flirting with me. I'm just saying I'm not good at this and I don't know what flirting is exactly. I think he was just trying to be nice, that's all."

"I get it," Ethan says. "Really, I do. Don't worry about it."

"Ethan..."

I guess that's it for now. We walk the rest of the way in silence. I don't know what to say to him. I don't want to argue with him, I just want to talk to him and explain everything to him but I don't feel comfortable doing it out in the open like this. I wish we were back home so that we could talk alone in the privacy of my bedroom or his, or in the car out for a drive, or anywhere.

I don't know. I really don't.

9 - Ethan

I CAN'T EVEN FUCKING... I don't know. I just can't even. There's nothing more to it than that.

This shit doesn't make sense. Am I not good enough for her? Does she want Caleb or something? To date him? And what the fuck is up with that "I don't know what flirting" is bullshit? How can she not know what flirting us? I seriously can't even comprehend that statement.

It's like saying she doesn't know how to breathe. We all know how to breathe, Princess. It's kind of an essential part of life.

What if she really doesn't know what flirting is, though? Shit. I'm an asshole, then, huh? It seems like something everyone knows, but maybe she's right. I do have a lot more experience than her. Is that bad? Does she feel like, uh... does she think it's bad?

I don't exactly think it's good, but I can't change any of that, now can I? Nah, not really. Sort of, but I don't like that idea.

I can't have *less* experience, but she can have *more*. Thinking about it pisses me off, though, angry as fuck.

Whatever. I'm done with this. I don't want to think about it anymore.

That's what I tell myself, except I keep thinking about it, can't stop dwelling on it, and all through dinner I'm just super fucking pissed and I'm pretty sure everyone can tell. Ashley and her mom are whispering to each other about something, I don't even know. Ashley's mom talks to my dad, and he nods.

You know what I do? Roast some fucking hot dogs and eat them. We have a bag of chips, too. Real traditional campground food right here, nothing crazy. I eat and get pissed off more, and eat more, and... yeah.

It's a never-ending cycle, I guess. The circle of fucking life over here, except I guess it's actually just the circle of me being pissed off. Yeah yeah, I'm used to it. I used to be an angry kid, too. I thought I was over it a long time ago, but I guess not.

Everyone's done. We're clearing up. The fire is down to regular levels, just crackling, nice and warm but not super bright. Ashley takes off and heads to the tent.

"Are you sure you don't want to share a tent with your mom?" my dad asks.

Fuck off, Dad. Seriously, just go fuck off. I don't mean to call my own dad a dick, but right now he's being a dick.

"No, it's fine," Ashley says, smiling. "Thank you, though."

She unzips the tent, but before she gets in, she smiles at me, too. Waves a little.

Yeah... good night, Princess. Sorry. I love you...

"Hey, can we talk for a second?" my dad says to me as soon as Ashley's zipped up in the tent.

"Yeah sure," I say.

He gets up. I guess we're going for a walk in the woods or something, some father and son bonding time.

Or not. Fuck.

"What are you doing?" my dad asks. "Caleb seems nice. You need to leave him and Ashley alone. Let them have fun and get to know each other."

Can he say anything worse than that right now? If he can, I don't know what it would be. Seriously, no fucking clue, and I'm pretty sure that's the worst. I don't want to hear this shit.

"We're only going to be here for a week or two," I remind him, trying to be logical here. How does Ashley do it? Fuck if I know. "It's not like anything serious can happen."

"Who said anything about serious?" my dad asks. "That's how long you always spent with your girl of the week, isn't it? You seem to have figured out how to have fun and spend time with them given a limited timeframe."

Wow. Holy fucking wow. Did he really just say that? Fuck!

"She deserves better, Dad," I say, trying to calm down. I'm seeing red, though. It's dark as fuck and we're in the middle of the woods and the only thing I can see is bright fucking red.

"It's not up to you to decide what Ashley deserves. She can make her own decisions. Maybe this is good for her, too. I don't know. Breakups are always hard, and sometimes rebound relationships like this can help. You of all people should understand that relationships don't always have to be serious, Ethan."

"Yeah, I guess so," I say.

It's true, right? Who the fuck am I to fight against my own past. I never treated anything serious before. I was the rebound relationship guy more than once. I liked being that guy. I liked showing girls a good time, helping them get over their shitty relationships with asshole douchebags, and then moving on to do it again.

I can rationalize it all I want, but it doesn't change what I did.

Well, fuck.

"Just let it play out," my dad says. "For all we know, nothing's going to happen. Ashley might not even like him. If so, that's fine, but don't force her away from him, alright? Let it happen on its own. Got it?"

Fuck you, Dad. "Yeah, got it."

We head back to the campsite again. Ashley's mom is sitting by the fire, packing up some of our leftovers, bagging the trash.

"You look tired," she says to me. "Maybe you should get some sleep?"

"You sure you don't need help?" I ask.

"There's not a lot," she says, smiling. "Go, go. Have a good night, Ethan."

I don't know what that smile is about. Maybe she doesn't realize what the fuck is going on here. I sure do. I hear it loud and clear.

I go to the tent I'm sharing with Ashley, unzip it, and step inside. Our sleeping bags are all set up, plus our bags with our clothes are stuffed away in the back, pillows and shit, all our things. Her shoes are by the front flap, and I take mine off to leave them there, too.

Before I zip up the tent, I look down at her. She's huddled in her sleeping bag, with only her face visible, holding the top tight against her with her hands. She's watching me. Uh... hey to you, too, Princess?

I don't fucking know. I zip the tent up and settle down. I think I'm settling down, at least, getting into my sleeping bag, but before I can, she sweeps back the top of her sleeping bag and uh...

Holy shit. No, for real, *holy shit*.

She's got sleepwear on, I guess you could call it. And by that I mean it's some sexy as fuck skimpy lingerie. I don't know what this shit's called, I just like to look at it. It's white and thin enough to see through, with little spaghetti straps around her shoulders, and a slim piece of lace fabric covering her breasts, and her stomach, down to the middle of her body. That's about where that ends. What the fuck do you call this? Negligee or teddy or something?

I don't know, but I can't stop staring. She's got a matching pair of white panties, too. I can't see through those, but I can basically see through the rest. It's kind of dark, but the campfire gives me enough light to fully enjoy and appreciate her body.

Yeah, there's a lot of appreciation going on right about now.

Seriously, holy shit.

Ashley reaches out for my hand, taking it in hers. We hold hands for a few seconds, just soft and nice like that, then she brings my hand to the bottom of her negligee. I touch the lace and her skin, just letting my fingers enjoy her. She moves my hand up under her lingerie, then up more. I move with her, tracing my palm along her stomach, then to her breasts. When I have one hand on her breast, I just... yeah, I've got two hands and her other breast looks lonely, so...

I sweep the other hand up her stomach to her other breasts, and cup them both in my palms, fingers squeezing her soft, beautiful curves. She closes her eyes and parts her lips, almost letting out a light moan, but I stop her with my mouth, kissing her. Quiet, though. Our parents are right outside, and I know they're still awake. This is kind of fucking dangerous, Princess. I don't know what you're trying to start here, but I really do want to finish it, it's just...

I move down closer to her, joining her in the sleeping bag. I just now realize that she's zipped the bottoms of our sleeping bags together. Real fucking subtle, huh? Apparently she doesn't even care. We're sleeping together and cuddling whether I want to or not.

I really fucking want to. Really really want to.

I just need to know something first. I need to let her know something first.

I can hear my dad and Ashley's mom talking by the fire. I need to do this quietly. I kiss her cheek, then whisper to her.

"Can I talk to you about something?" I ask.

"What?" she whispers back.

"You know me, right? I know you do, and part of that is knowing that I've uh... look, let's just be real for a second. I feel like an asshole for bringing this up, but I've slept with a lot of girls."

She stiffens slightly. My hands are still on her breasts and I almost take them away, because I don't want to do this like that. I'm basically on top of her right now, or almost on top of her, and here I am talking about other girls when uh...

Yeah, the lingerie is amazing. I honestly didn't expect that.

"What are you trying to say?" she asks me. "Ethan, you can talk to me about anything. You know that, right?"

"I know that's one of our rules," I tell her. "I'm trying to be open with you, but this is hard. Just give me a second, alright?"

She turns to kiss me quickly, then nods. "Alright."

I gather my composure or whatever the fuck I'm supposed to be doing. Never thought I'd be saying something like this ever, but I guess I never thought I'd be in a situation like this, either. It's not easy. It's really fucking difficult, actually.

"I never really thought about it before, but I have a lot more experience than you," I tell her. "I know you haven't been with a lot of guys. Maybe it's like your missing out or something. I don't know. Do you want to have a fling with Caleb? Just a week or two or whatever, however long we're here. Sex and shit. Casual as fuck. I'd be super fucking jealous and honestly kind of pissed off, but I'll deal with it. If you think you need more experiences or something, then I don't want you to regret being with me and feeling like you're missing out. It'd just be a week or two. I think I can handle that. It's not like I want to, but I'm just giving you the option here, Princess. I just..."

Fuck. I can't keep going. She can make up her mind and tell me. Now, tomorrow morning, whatever. We're here for awhile.

A part of me wants her to do it. It's not like I want her sleeping with that fuck, but he's probably a decent looking guy and maybe it's good for her. For fuck's sake, she's never even had a fling before. I've had like... a lot. I don't even know. I'd rather not think about it right now.

The rest of me doesn't even want to have this conversation, though. I don't want to think about ever having it, but I just started it, so we're having it.

I feel like shit. I seriously want to go outside and throw up right now.

"You know what?" she says to me, soft and smiling.

"What?"

"That's how we got into this mess in the first place, isn't it? Saying it'd just be a week?"

I roll my eyes at her and laugh a little, but I try to stay quiet because of her mom and my dad outside. They're still talking to each other, so I don't think they've heard us. We've just been whispering and shit, so I think we're good.

"I don't want to have a fling with Caleb," she says. "I don't want to have a fling with anyone. I do want to catch up with your experience level, Ethan, but is it alright if I just do it with you? I take back the fling thing. I do want to have flings, but I want to have them with you only. A lot of them, over and over."

"I don't think that's a fling, Princess," I say, grinning at her. "That sounds like a long term relationship."

"Maybe," she says, grinning back at me. "It's like a really long fling with a lot of benefits."

"I love benefits," I tell her.

"Just with me?" she asks, coy.

"Yeah, only you," I say.

"Show me?"

Yeah, uh... you think I'm going to turn that down? She wants more experience? I'll give it to her. I want to give her that so much, you don't even fucking know.

I push her legs apart a little more with my knees. My hands are still on her breasts, and I squeeze them lightly, massaging her with my fingers. I caress and squeeze her curves, then kiss her. Her mouth first, then her neck, down to the center of her breasts, further down to her stomach.

This negligee is really short. It barely covers more than the tops of her thighs. I don't want it to cover any more than that, though. Also, these panties are in the way. I push up her lace lingerie and kiss her belly button, then a little lower. I move my hands from her breasts to her hips. Grabbing the center of her white panties with my fingers, I slip them to the side, exposing her bare sex.

I don't know what I expected to find here. I mean, I know what's going on, but it's just... just better. I don't know how, it just is.

It's dark and the fire is the only thing shining any light on our situation right now. We're far enough away where it's mostly shadow and dancing light, though. The shadows caress her body, mixing with the wetness between her legs. She looks so fucking beautiful and sexy right now.

I can't hold back. I seriously need to taste the fuck out of her. I'm going to die if I don't.

Careful, tentative as fuck, I slide my tongue from the bottom of her pussy all the way to the top. She's delicious and sweet, aroused and wet. For me. Just me. Yeah, I could get used to that. I don't want to get used to it, though. I want to savor this forever, never take her for granted.

"Is this rule number eleven?" she whispers to me, excited.

"You bet your fucking ass it is," I whisper back.

My tongue's not enough. I need more. I want to feel every inch of her body. I grab her thighs tight in my hands, squeezing her soft, sexy flesh. She lets out a light whimper of pleasure. Yeah, I like that. Music to my fucking ears, Princess. Give me more.

I squeeze one of her legs a little tighter and run my other hand up to the apex of her thighs. The panties I pulled aside earlier are going back to their regular position, which kind of fucks up this rule number eleven thing, don't you think? I fix that with my hand again, but then I fix it even more by dipping two fingers inside her. She squirms and writhes as soon as I enter her, and I make her wriggle even more by tapping the tip of my tongue against her clit.

Some guys focus on nipples to figure out a woman's arousal. Yeah, girls get wet, too, but I think other guys need to broaden their horizons a little. You know what else gets harder? Yeah, it's the thing right under my tongue. I tease and lap at her clit, sliding my tongue around the curves of her clitoral hood, pressing lightly against her.

I just want more. Is that too much to ask? I want her clit to throb in ecstasy, become so fucking overflowing with pleasure that I can feel her heart-beat pulsing through it. I want to pull and suck her clit into my mouth and feel it against my lips, pressing lightly against it with my teeth. I want to feel her cum with my mouth, feel her clit tremble and shiver.

I love watching that. I love it with Ashley. She's so responsive and beautiful, like she's giving me everything and all of her. You know what? I bet she is, too. She doesn't hold back, and I don't want to, either. Just take every fucking inch of me, Ashley. Every single piece, all of me. I'm yours, Princess. I just want the same thing in return.

I like watching the lips of her pussy quiver in excitement as I slide my fingers in and out of her. I can see her stomach clenching in anticipation. Letting go of her thigh, I move my hand up to her stomach. I can feel it now, too. I press slightly against her stomach and her pubis, savoring the sensation of her body.

I pull my fingers out of her and taste her again. How many fucking licks does it take to get to her liquid candy center? I don't know, but I want to find out. One, two, three...

She shivers beneath me. Yeah, uh... I'm as lost as you are, Princess. I want to get lost inside you, want to taste every beautiful part of you, work my way from the inside out. She's even more wet than before, so fucking aroused. I love it.

I think maybe we're both a little too lost, because uh...

You know who has the worst timing in the world? Yeah, it's my dad. Fuck.

"You two alright in there?" my dad asks.

The tent is closed, and he can't see in. I hope to fuck he doesn't unzip it for who knows what reason. I need my privacy here, Dad. Go away. I'm busy. So is Ashley. We've got orgasms to attend to.

Ashley whimpers, lost in ecstasy. Uh... I'm busy so I can't answer, either. I've got my mouth full of her juicy pussy. Do I really have to be the one to say something? I'd rather not. To be honest, I'm still kind of pissed off at my dad, too.

"Y-y-yessss," Ashley says.

I'm not sure if she's talking to my dad, or just letting me know what a good fucking job I'm doing. I kind of already know I'm good, though. Don't mean to be cocky there, but you should always own up to your accomplishments, you know?

"Alright," my dad says, hesitant. "We're going to go to sleep now, too. Figure we can get up early and work out our plans for the day that way. The fire's out, and everything's all set out here. It can get kind of cold at night, Ashley, so if you need a blanket, there are some in the car. If you have to go to the bathroom at night but you're scared, don't feel bad about waking up Ethan, either. You hear that, Ethan?"

I grunt. I'm not going to talk, I'm just going to grunt. That's what I usually do, so I think I'm good to do it now.

Also I double down on the feast in front of me. Holy fuck, she really is delicious. The perfect dessert. I just can't get enough of this...

"Do you need anything before I go to the tent?" my dad asks.

I'm about to stop what I'm doing and tell my dad exactly where he can go, and not even remotely politely, but before I can pull my head away, Ashley grabs fistfuls of my hair in her fingers and pulls me back towards her sweet center. Mmm... yeah, show me what you like, Princess. I lick and lap at her clit, thrusting two fingers inside her again.

"I'm fine! Really! I'm--" Ashley squeezes my head hard in her hand.

She's cumming. That's what she *"is"* right now. She's cumming.

My dad says something. Who the fuck knows what? I'm done with listening to him at the moment.

I feel Ashley's pussy clenching and squeezing against my fingers. I drive them in deep, then hook them up, pulling and raking against the beautiful fucking pleasure spot at the top of her pussy. I love it, love the feeling of it, love the roughness and the way her inner walls grip against my fingers like she's trying to pull them deeper inside of her.

I want to be inside of her. I want to bury my cock in her, feel her orgasm tightening around my shaft. Later, though. I've got to finish this first. I want to show her a world of pleasure, give her every fucking experience she could ever imagine.

I don't know how long we're like that. My neck kind of hurts right now, but I just want to keep licking and sucking on her clit. I want to keep feeling her clenching in orgasm around my fingers. She's done, though. It's just little trembles now, soft squeezes, while she breathes heavily. She collapses against the ground, her hands falling loose from my head.

Yeah, I'm pretty fucking amazing like that. Don't even forget it.

I slip away from her, sliding up alongside her body. I can't see any of her anymore, it's too dark out, but I don't have to see her to know how beautiful she is right now. I wrap my arms around her and pull her close to me.

Why do I still have clothes on? Fuck if I know. I should really do something about that. Later, though. I just want to cuddle the fuck out of her right now, hold her tight, love her entirely. I need it more than I need to breathe.

Ashley giggles into my ear when I'm right next to her. She giggles and kisses me quick, then again, over and over.

"What's so funny?" I ask, grinning at her and kissing her back.

"Do you think this is what it means when a girl says that a guy makes her panties melt?" she asks me. "I think mine are kind of soaked right now. Definitely feels like they're melted."

"I don't know, Princess," I tell her. "Pretty fucking sure we can melt them a whole lot more than that. Want me to try?"

"Oh, yes..." she says. "But... can we just cuddle for a little while? Can you put your pajamas on and can we cuddle, Ethan? I love you."

"Yeah, we can do that," I say. "I love you, too, Princess."

I strip down and put on my pajama pants. I left them at the top of my bag, so it's pretty easy to find them. I toss on a shirt quick, too. Then cuddling. Fuck, I love to cuddle with her.

It's still cuddling if my cock's inside her, right? Uh...

This isn't sex. Not yet. Maybe later. I don't care. I just want to be as close to her as I can possibly be. We're facing each other, my body pressed tight to hers. I pull her leg up and around my thigh, then I shift and move as close to her as possible. I pull down the top of my pajama pants, giving my erection free reign to roam a little. It's not going all that far away, though, don't worry.

I grab my shaft and line myself up with her slit, then shift and move a little more, pushing inside of her. She lets out a soft gasp and kisses me while I figure all of this out. There. Yeah, that's good.

We cuddle like that, my cock throbbing inside her, both of us kissing. I hold her tight, face to face.

We'll have sex. We're going to. Sort of. Soft and sweet and nice. I'm going to make love to her. I do love her. I love every fucking part of her. Soon we'll make love, but not now. We're just cuddling right now.

"I don't know if we can wake up early," I tell her. "I want to stay up all night."

"Oh? Doing what?" she asks, coy.

"Worshiping your existence," I say.

"Awww..."

"With my cock."

She laughs a little too loud, then covers her mouth with her hands. "Ethan! You can't say things like that. It's weird."

"Nah, it's the truth."

"It just sounds weird," she says. "I don't think you're supposed to say it like that."

"I was trying to be romantic and sweet as fuck," I tell her.

"That's the kind of thing I mean," she says. "You can say you're trying to be romantic and sweet, but as soon as you add the 'as fuck' at the end, it kind of um... loses its original meaning, don't you think?"

"Listen, Princess." Time to tell it to her straight. Serious talk right here. "I can't think about anything when I'm inside you. It feels too good."

"How good?" she asks, wiggling her hips. My cock slides in and out of her a little. Mmm-yeah...

"So good," I tell her. "A million times more, exponentially or something. There's too much math involved to figure it out, I can't even tell you."

"Is it the best?" she asks me. "Be truthful, please? I just... I want to know. I won't be upset if it's not."

"You think I'm lying?" I ask her, smiling. "I'm being serious, Ashley. You're amazing. You're smart, and funny, and a lot of fun, but you're also sexy as fuck and I'm being completely honest when I say the best sex I've ever had has been with you. Not just once or twice, so you know it's not a fluke or anything. Every fucking time is better than the last. I don't even know how the fuck this works. I didn't think shit like that was possible before I was with you."

"Really?" she asks.

I kiss her just to feel her smile against my lips. "Really," I say.

"I love you so much, Ethan."

"I love you, too, beautiful."

I think this is going to be a long night. I'm going to be tired in the morning. She might be, too. We're going to have to find a way to take a nap or something, except I'm pretty sure if you leave me alone in a room with this girl, or alone in a tent, whatever, uh... yeah, I need her. I need all of her, everything about her.

I'll figure out what we're going to do tomorrow when it's tomorrow. Right now I want to love her and make love to her. Nothing else matters. This is the most important thing I can think of.

A NOTE FROM MIA

OH NO! There's a little more trouble brewing in paradise...

I think the addition of Caleb's character is interesting, especially with the strange push from Ethan's dad. I guess it doesn't help that Ashley isn't exactly sure what to do, either. It's an interesting situation and I think it will get more interesting, too. Ashley's never really had attention from many boys before, because she's got her head buried in books and studying. It's not like that's unattractive exactly, but if a lot of guys at college want a girl who will go out and party with them or whatever, um... that's not really the type of thing Ashley is into.

Caleb doesn't even know what sort of girl she is, though. Also Caleb doesn't know that she's dating Ethan. And Ethan's dad still doesn't know. I'm not sure this is going to go well for them. It seems like everything's going to bubble up to the top sooner rather than later and then...

Well, we'll see how it goes! I think it will be exciting.

Ashley and her mom are dangerous, too. I thought they were supposed to be the good girls here? Haha. The tent ripping scheme... definitely not something a good girl would usually do. That's alright, though. I think it's good to take a walk on the wild side sometimes, right? It certainly paid off for her this first night, and there's many more where that came from.

I just wanted to add a little more intrigue and drama to this part, though. There's a little more coming, and it's all going to build up until... well, I can't tell you that! It's a secret, but I think you will enjoy what I have planned. It should be fun.

Thank you for reading, and I hope you're really enjoying this season so far! We're at about the halfway point right now, but there's still a lot of excitement planned for the next few episodes. If you liked this one, I'd love if you could leave me a review. I really appreciate it a ton, and I love hearing everyone's nice thoughts and kind words.

Bye for now!

~MIA

ABOUT THE AUTHOR

Mia likes to have fun in all aspects of her life. Whether she's out enjoying the beautiful weather or spending time at home reading a book, a smile is never far from her face. She's prone to randomly laughing at nothing in particular except for whatever idea amuses her at any given moment.

Sometimes you just need to enjoy life, right?

She loves to read, dance, and explore outdoors. Chamomile tea and bubble baths are two of her favorite things. Flowers are especially nice, and she could get lost in a garden if it's big enough and no one's around to remind her that there are other things to do.

She lives in New Hampshire, where the weather is beautiful and the autumn colors are amazing.

Made in the USA
San Bernardino, CA
26 March 2017